"Let me see—you don't like to say 'Merry Christmas'…"

He pulled his chin away, but she cupped his strong jaw and kept him facing her. The late-night shadow of his beard was scraggly and dark and added an air of menace to him.

"You don't like anyone hinting that you're a good cop who KCPD could still use, and you don't like admitting when you have feelings for someone." Holly stroked her thumb across his lips. *This* guy made her toes curl inside her socks and brace for trouble.

The elevator hit a gentle bump and slowed its descent. "Am I pretty clear as to what your words are telling me?"

He opened his mouth, about to deny the truth.

Instead, he reawakened his dragon's heart with another kiss….

JULIE MILLER

KANSAS CITY CHRISTMAS

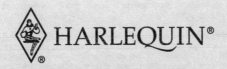

HARLEQUIN®

TORONTO • NEW YORK • LONDON
AMSTERDAM • PARIS • SYDNEY • HAMBURG
STOCKHOLM • ATHENS • TOKYO • MILAN • MADRID
PRAGUE • WARSAW • BUDAPEST • AUCKLAND

For the Class of 1978. Fulton High School, Fulton, Missouri.

Happy Anniversary to us. Anytime a place can take
a shy girl and give her a place to shine, a place to be
inspired by talented, dedicated teachers, and a place
to make dear, lifelong friends and memories—
you know it's a good place.

Thank you.

Recycling programs
for this product may
not exist in your area.

ISBN-13: 978-0-373-88873-3
ISBN-10:   0-373-88873-2

KANSAS CITY CHRISTMAS

ABOUT THE AUTHOR

Julie Miller attributes her passion for writing romance to all those fairy tales she read growing up, and shyness. Encouragement from her family to write down all those feelings she couldn't express became a love for the written word. She gets continued support from her fellow members of the Prairieland Romance Writers, where she serves as the resident "grammar goddess." This award-winning author and teacher has published several paranormal romances. Inspired by the likes of Agatha Christie and Encyclopedia Brown, Ms. Miller believes the only thing better than a good mystery is a good romance.

Born and raised in Missouri, she now lives in Nebraska with her husband, son and smiling guard dog, Maxie. Write to Julie at P.O. Box 5162, Grand Island, NE 68802-5162.

Books by Julie Miller

HARLEQUIN INTRIGUE

841—POLICE BUSINESS*
880—FORBIDDEN CAPTOR
898—SEARCH AND SEIZURE*
947—BABY JANE DOE*
966—BEAST IN THE TOWER
1009—UP AGAINST THE WALL**
1015—NINE-MONTH PROTECTOR**
1070—PROTECTIVE INSTINCTS†
1073—ARMED AND DEVASTATING†
1090—PRIVATE S.W.A.T TAKEOVER†
1099—KANSAS CITY CHRISTMAS†

*The Precinct
**The Precinct: Vice Squad
†The Precinct: Brotherhood of the Badge

CAST OF CHARACTERS

Edward Kincaid—A burnt-out, beat-up KCPD legend with nothing left to lose. He doesn't believe he's anybody's last hope, though a bossy, beautiful criminalist seems to think so.

Dr. Holly Masterson, M.E.—Criminalist with the KCPD crime lab—just as smart as her legs are long. When evidence starts disappearing from her lab and a mysterious stalker threatens her reputation and her life, is the danger personal? Or part of one of the biggest cover-ups in Kansas City history?

Rick Temple—Holly's coworker. A CSI with a weird sense of humor.

Jillian Masterson—Holly's younger sister. Trouble seems to have a way of finding her.

Blake Rivers—Jillian's on-again, off-again boyfriend. He works at Caldwell Technologies.

William Caldwell—Longtime Kincaid family friend. Could someone in his own company be responsible for his best friend's murder?

Hayley Resnick—Television reporter. Does she know the answers before she asks the questions?

Irina Zorinsky Hansford—Back from the dead after thirty years? Or is someone exacting vengeance in her name?

Kevin Grove—Homicide detective leading the investigation into John Kincaid's murder.

Z Group—A covert organization disbanded at the end of the Cold War. Or are they still in business? And who is willing to kill to keep their secrets?

John Kincaid—Will his sons finally uncover his killer?

Chapter One

April

"…And I will sleep in peace until you come to me."

"I hope you find peace, Dad." Edward Kincaid turned away from the funeral service in the distance and limped back up the sloping hill of Mt. Washington Cemetery to his own hell. It wasn't the first time he'd been to a ceremony to bury a fellow cop. But it was the first time he'd shown up for one without wearing his own uniform or badge. And it was the first time he'd shown up to bury his own father. "I don't know how. But I hope you do."

Edward couldn't feel the cold rain seeping through his hair and running down his scalp. But he felt the chill of the April day down in his knitted bones. He could barely make out the lyrics of the song his youngest brother, Holden, was singing. But he felt the mournful melody deep in his soul.

His mother and brothers, colleagues from the

KCPD and more family friends than he could count were gathered on the opposite side of the copse of evergreens and ash trees to his back. But here were the only two people he wanted to be with right now. With his cane sinking into the mud, he awkwardly knelt down in front of the pink marble gravestone and wiped the rain away from the words carved there.

Beloved Wife. Beloved Daughter.

Cara and Melinda Kincaid. He should be in the ground beside them. Instead of them.

Tears burned in his eyes, but he didn't shed them. He was all cried out months ago.

He heard the minister talking. He'd gotten this far. If he was going to do this thing, if he was going to face those mourners, he'd better get moving.

"I can't stay today, girls," he whispered. The thick, moist air swallowed up the gravelly rasp of his voice. "But I wanted... I wanted you to know that I'm sober today. I'm doing it for Dad. I wish I'd been strong enough to get my act together for you. I'm going to do right by him—by you, too. I threw out the bottles the night I got the call about...his murder. That's five days sober. I'm going to make it one more." One day at a time was what his AA sponsor kept telling him. One day was about all he had in him anymore. "I promise."

Melinda would have jumped up and thrown herself into his arms to congratulate him. Despite her young age and her disability, his daughter had always been intuitive about moods. She knew when her daddy needed a hug, when he needed to be left alone, and when he needed someone to cheer him on and make him smile.

Five days without a drink wasn't much for a man who'd been trying to numb his brain and heart since Christmas Eve, the first anniversary of their deaths. But Melinda's pure love would have made him feel as though five days was the entire world. Cara would have been a little more low-key about the whole thing, saying something that would keep him from getting a big head about his accomplishment. And later, she'd find a way to congratulate him privately, personally—and very thoroughly. His two girls would have inspired him to live better than he had been, try harder than he knew how, feel more than he'd ever thought possible.

If only his wife and daughter were still with him. He didn't want to be at the cemetery. He didn't want to accept another death—especially not this one. He didn't want to feel a damn thing.

But he owed his father a hell of a lot more than drinking himself stupid and not showing up for his funeral.

"I want you to look for Grandpa, angel." Leaning heavily on his cane, Edward pushed himself up to his feet. "Grandpa's coming to see you, he missed you so much. Give him a hug."

His canvas jacket was soaked and clinging to his shoulders before he could finally tear himself away from the memories and guilt. But once his mind was back in the present, Edward turned his ear toward the ceremony continuing just thirty yards or so behind him. Holden had finished his song, and KCPD's lady commissioner was speaking now, eulogizing his father. "Deputy Commissioner John Kincaid was the finest example of what being a Kansas City police officer is all about."

Edward nodded in silent agreement and cut through the trees to study the sea of umbrellas and listen to the remainder of the service. The world itself was weeping at the injustice of the day. John Kincaid had inspired him to join KCPD. He'd taught Edward how to be a cop, a man, and a father— teaching by example. Edward had already lost more than he could stand when his wife and daughter were murdered. How was he supposed to deal with his father being beaten and shot to death as well?

The world made no sense. What was the point of following the rules and fighting for justice and giving a damn when the bad guys still won?

Back when he'd been an active-duty investigator and undercover cop for KCPD, he'd dealt with violence and death nearly every day, but he'd been able to remain detached and focused enough to get his job done. But then he'd lost Cara and Melinda, and death had become an inescapable, personal, destructive demon. Now his father, a good man—the man he'd once aspired to be—had been murdered as well.

How many pieces of his soul did a man have in him to lose?

Commissioner Shauna Cartwright finished her eulogy, and the blue KCPD uniforms all bowed their heads for the minister's closing prayer. The twenty-one gun salute visibly jolted through his mother, Susan Kincaid, whom he could see sitting between two of his brothers—Atticus and Holden. His brothers wore their full dress KCPD uniforms with black mourning ribbons draped across the badges on their chests. He searched beyond the green awning to find his next eldest brother, Sawyer, standing hatless in the rain. He wore KCPD dress as well. Sawyer stood next to William Caldwell, one of their family's oldest friends. Bill was leaning in, offering some condolence or words of wisdom that Sawyer would hear but not take, especially if the words involved *patience* or *let someone else handle this.* Bill Caldwell was like an uncle to them—having been a fraternity brother of their father's and fishing buddy before any of John Kincaid's sons were even born.

Edward was looking at a family in stoic devastation. It wasn't a world that he'd ever wanted to welcome them to.

"What the…?" Edward pulled his shoulders back and stood a little taller. "Don't do this, Atticus."

It was one thing to feel the emptiness and injustice of the day. It was another to have to put words to it and deal with anybody else's pain. But his brother had broken away from the gathering and was striding straight toward him.

Atticus's gray eyes matched his, as determined to have this conversation as Edward wished he could avoid it. Stubborn son of a gun. Atticus wasn't a man he could glare away. Not if the proffered hand was any indication.

"Don't tell me you don't recognize what this means, Edward. It's good to see you."

The idea of turning around and walking away remained a distinct possibility. But the idea of explaining his cowardice to Cara or Melinda, who rested only a few yards away, was even more untenable. So he reached out and shook Atticus's hand, grudgingly reconnecting with his family. Grief and anger and understanding passed between them. "Don't you dare try to hug me."

Atticus almost laughed at his grinch-like reply. But this wasn't a day for laughter. Instead, his younger brother turned and stood beside him, watching as friends and family dispersed, ducking under umbrellas and walking down the hill toward their cars.

They stood together, like the old days, back when John Kincaid's four sons had been invincible. Those days were long gone—for Edward, at least. The soft patter of the rain on the overhanging trees should have been a soothing sound. But Edward heard each plop against every branch like the ticking of a clock. Atticus didn't do anything without a purpose, and he seriously doubted that this reunion was just a "Hey—how are you doing?"moment.

"You should come say hi to Mom. She knows you're here, but it'd mean a lot to her if you made the effort to touch base." He should have suspected Atticus's mission before he spoke. "She's hurting. We all are."

Welcome to my hell.

But it was a sentiment he would never utter aloud to his grieving brother. Edward inhaled a deep breath and tried to say something appropriately sympathetic. "I'm sure Mom has invited people over to the house, but I can't do the small-talk thing. Just give her my love."

"Give it to her yourself. Let me get Sawyer and Holden on this. We'll keep everyone away and you can have a private moment with her before she leaves Mt. Washington."

"Atticus, I…" *Grandma needs a hug, too.* Edward ducked his head and turned away as his daughter's sweet voice tormented his conscience.

He could wallow in grief and anger all he wanted. But he'd never been able to say no to his little girl.

His mother needed him right now. His family

needed him. Edward had nothing left to give, nothing left to say. But for Cara and Melinda—and for John Kincaid—he'd find the strength to at least go through the motions. He'd find the caring that had been gutted from him somewhere along the way.

"I'll meet you by her car in ten minutes."

"WHEN I GAVE YOU BOYS literary names, I didn't think you'd take them to heart." Susan Kincaid, dedicated English teacher and loving wife and mother, patted Edward's knee as she scooted closer beside him in the rear seat of the funeral home's limousine, still parked on the road that twisted through Mt. Washington cemetery. "Edward Rochester Kincaid—just like Jane Eyre's Mr. Rochester—you've been burned so badly by the world that you feel your only comfort is to hide away from it. He didn't find peace until he was forced from his seclusion by Jane. He didn't understand how much he was loved and needed, either." Resting one hand on the folded American flag that sat in her lap, she reached over and laced her fingers together with Edward's. "These are hellish circumstances to force you from your seclusion. But I'm so glad you're here, son. It…soothes me."

Soothing? Edward was shaking inside his skin with raw emotion and the uncertainty about what he should—and could—do to help his family through this tragedy.

Cocooned by the rain and three younger brothers who stood guard outside the long black car to ensure their privacy, the limo's plush interior absorbed the scoffing noise Edward made. He breathed in his mother's subtle perfume along with the musty dampness that clung to their clothes and took note of the slight tremor in her chilled fingers as they nested inside his broader, callused, scarred-up hand. He'd never been given much to romantic notions, not even before a killer bent on revenge had torn his life apart.

A year and a half ago Edward had been a damn good cop, one of the best undercover operatives KCPD's drug enforcement division had ever put on the streets. Edward and his team had worked months to put one of Kansas City's top cocaine suppliers out of business. Yet a technicality had allowed André Butler to walk away after a mistrial. Sure, Butler's empire had been destroyed, his sources outed. But until a second trial could be mounted, the self-proclaimed modern gangster had walked out of the courthouse a free man—a free man looking for payback against the cop he'd trusted like a brother—a brother who had ultimately betrayed him.

Butler had been released on December twenty-third. His first stop after spending the night with a girlfriend and stealing her car the next morning? Edward's front yard. According to witnesses,

Melinda had been building a snowman that day, keeping herself busy while Cara loaded presents into the car for the Kincaids' traditional Christmas Eve get-together at his parents' home. Butler had lured Melinda out to the street, shot Cara when she tried to protect their trusting little girl and then shot Melinda to silence her wailing cries over her fallen mother. Edward had been out to pick up a bicycle with training wheels for Melinda's Christmas present when he got the call about Butler being spotted near his own address. He'd raced and skidded over slushy, snow-packed streets in a desperate effort to get to his family.

By the time he turned the corner onto his block, Edward knew he was already too late. Butler ran to his car, turning his gun on Edward's speeding SUV and firing off multiple shots. Edward prayed the bastard's neck hadn't snapped when he ran him down—that he'd died a slow, painful death. Though he'd barely felt it at the time, one of the bullets had cracked his windshield and pierced his chest, doing plenty of damage to his insides. Plowing over Butler, crashing through a line of parked cars and wrapping his engine around a tree had done even more. With both legs busted and his own blood leaving a crimson trail across the snow, Edward had crawled to the front sidewalk to try to breathe life back into the women he loved.

He'd taken out the bad guy, but he couldn't save them.

Merry Christmas.

Yeah, any romantic notions he might have once had were long gone.

"Edward?"

His mother's grip steadied as her soft voice jerked him back to the present. Why had he gone back to that morning? Too many beers had numbed his memory for too many months. But now that the physical mess of reclaiming sobriety had passed, every detail of that morning—every image, every hurt, every blame—stuck in his head with painful clarity.

He had no business being here, no business making this day any worse for his family than it already was. "Mom, I…"

Edward tried to withdraw his hand, but Susan held on tight.

He stared down at their interlocking fingers, resting atop his thigh. He was supposed to say something now. Unlike smooth-talking Holden, or Atticus who'd always been smart enough to figure out what needed to be said, or even Sawyer, who led with his heart and blazed ahead and dealt with the consequences later, Edward wished he was eloquent enough to either compliment his mother's strength or console her grief. But his instincts about such things were rusty from months of lonely isolation, and the right words wouldn't come.

They didn't have to. Susan Kincaid hadn't been married to a cop or raised four more for nothing. "I understand that you're not ready to face a crowd of well-wishers. I'm sure the comparisons to Cara and Melinda's funerals must be overwhelming. But it means everything to me that you made the effort to be here. For your family."

Was simply showing up really enough? He turned his head and looked down into the sincerity shining from her dark eyes. No wonder his father had loved this woman so much. Edward leaned over and kissed her cheek. "Atticus can be pretty darn convincing."

Susan stroked the neat, triangular flag that had been draped over his father's coffin. Stress and sorrow had deepened the crow's feet beside her eyes as she summoned a smile. "He doesn't take no for an answer, does he."

"Never has."

"He's stubborn, like your father. Smart like him, too." Her smile faded into a wistful sigh. "Each of you has something of your father in him."

Edward absently twirled his dark walnut cane in his right hand in the heavy silence that followed. He was more steel pins than bone from the waist down, his heart and soul gutted. What part of John Kincaid did he have left in him?

His mother didn't need to be intuitive to sense his discomfort. She leaned her cheek into his shoulder.

"Holden obviously looks like your father—sings like him and has some of that Kincaid Irish charm in him, too. Sawyer has his heart—his gentleness, his compassion—he's just as eager to right the wrongs of the world as your father was. And you…?"

When she paused, Edward made a sound inside his chest that might once have been a laugh. "Hard to come up with something nice to say about me?"

"No. Hard to choose the right words to say so that you'll believe them." She turned in the seat to face him. "You're the leader of this family now—"

"No."

He shrugged away from her grasp and tried to retreat, but she simply followed him across the seat. "I know we're all grown-ups. Your brothers are fine men and can take care of themselves. They've been taking care of *me* these past five days."

His mother deserved better than an absentee son during a time like this. He should have been stronger. He should have been able to deal with this. "I'm sorry, Mom. I should have called. I was busy—"

"Coming to grips with the loss of yet another person you love." Laced with a gentle understanding he didn't deserve, the touch of her hand against his jaw was almost painful. "You were busy getting sober."

For a moment, his eyes locked onto hers. "How…?"

Her pale mouth curved into a smile. "Your clothes

smell clean. You trimmed that ratty beard. Your beautiful eyes are clear."

"So I'm a bum who ignored my own mother in her time of need." He turned away from her forgiving touch and intuitive gaze. "And you think *I'm* the leader of this family?"

She brushed her fingers across his jaw again, ignoring his sardonic tone. "Your father would be so proud of you today."

He could pull away from the gentle touch, ignore the kind words. But the sheen of tears pooling in her eyes and spilling over did him in. Edward caught the first tear with the pad of his thumb and wiped the trail of sorrow from her cheek. "Mom…I… What are we supposed to do? Just because I'm the oldest doesn't mean I can make sense of any of this. I can't make this right."

"But you can make it better. You *have* made it better, just by being here."

"In a way, I can see one good thing about the girls not being here—I don't know how I'd explain losing Dad to Melinda. She loved her granddaddy so much. I'm not eight and I wasn't born with Down's syndrome. And I *still* don't understand this."

"They were crazy about each other, weren't they? John always called Melinda his little angel." Susan Kincaid leaned her cheek into Edward's hand. "I hadn't remembered that. That's a comfort to know they'll be together again." Wishing he had a handkerchief, Edward brushed away the new fall of tears. "Oh, Edward. I miss him so much."

Some comfort. His mother reached for him, caught him around the waist and hugged him tight. Edward reacted before he realized what the gesture might cost him. He wrapped his arms around her and held her close as his brittle defenses crumbled and her grief and confusion and anger flowed into his. "Just cry it on out, Mom. Just cry it out."

Several minutes passed before her sobbing sounds became erratic sniffles and then softened into steadier, more even breaths. His shirtfront was damp and streaked with her makeup as she finally pulled away. Her face became lined with a frown of confusion as her fingers probed the front waistband of his slacks. "You're not wearing your badge."

His KCPD badge was locked in a metal box with his guns, gathering dust on the back shelf of his closet until he could decide if he would ever be ready to be a cop again. But that wasn't what she wanted to hear. Kincaids were cops. The call to protect and serve was in their blood. That call had taken everything Edward loved. Today wasn't the day to explain his guilt, however. A logical excuse would serve well enough. "I've been on leave since a year ago Christmas."

Confusion briefly morphed into maternal concern. "Your doctor cleared you to go back on duty, right?"

"If I tended to my physical therapy the way I'm supposed to, then yeah, the doc says I could build up my strength and pass the physical. But I just don't think I can…." He squeezed his fist around the brass carving on his cane. The stick of heavy walnut had become a mental crutch as much as an aid for the physical pain that would never completely leave his rebuilt joints. Images of Cara's golden hair and Melinda's effervescent smile blipped through his mind. His last mental snapshot of his family had seen that golden hair matted with blood and his daughter's face lying pale and expressionless against the snow. He squeezed his eyes shut and tried to forget. But the task proved impossible, and he jerked his eyes open at his mother's gentle touch on his face.

"Shh." Susan Kincaid stroked his cheek and hair as though he was her little boy again, and she could soothe his hurts away with a maternal magic that somehow managed to salvage some pride while still making him feel better. Though this was no skinned knee they were dealing with today. "I'm not asking you to do anything you're not ready for. I have plenty enough to worry about on my plate. Your brothers are set on investigating your father's murder themselves."

"That doesn't surprise me." Sixteen months ago, he'd have been leading the pack to find the killer himself. "Don't worry about them, Mom. The department has protocols in place. They won't be able to play any official role in the case."

She arched one eyebrow as she pulled her hand away. "It's their *unofficial* curiosity that concerns me. We all want to find the killer, we all want justice. But I don't want to lose anyone else in the process—I don't want this to impact their careers or their lives any more than it already has."

Edward nodded. "You want me to talk some sense into them? I don't know that they'll listen to me."

"They'll listen. They look up to you, son. They trust your wisdom about the world."

"Mom, I—"

"Shh." She pressed her fingers against his mouth, refusing to hear his protest. Right. He was the leader of the family now. Man, were they screwed. "Just…remind them to keep their wits about them. And to watch their backs."

His eyes settled on a strand of gray hair that had fallen over her cheek. The gray hadn't been there the last time he'd seen her. The woman who'd been the Rock of Gibraltar for them throughout their lives was more vulnerable, more fragile than Edward had ever imagined. An inevitable sense of resignation— that call to duty that he'd tried to drink into a coma— awoke inside him. It was grouchy and unsure—and maybe even a bit afraid to take on the world again— but his mother's need had reawakened it.

Reaching out, Edward brushed the gray hair off her cheek and tucked it beneath the rich dark hair at her temple. "I'll talk to them. I'll help them however I can."

She blinked away another bout of tears and nodded her thanks. "And one more thing?" Why not? "I don't have your father's badge."

Edward tried to follow her unexpected tangent. Had it been buried with him? Did she want it back? Or had it simply been misplaced? "Where is it?" She shrugged. Okay. Not misplaced. "I'm sure the commissioner would issue a memorial copy—"

"No. You don't understand." Susan tugged at the front of Edward's coat, then quickly smoothed it back into place. "I want the badge he carried with him as a detective and deputy commissioner for all these years. It was never recovered from the crime scene. I don't know if it was lost during the struggle in the park when they kidnapped him from his morning run, or if one of those murderers kept it as some kind of souvenir."

Edward reached for his cane, certain that she was asking the wrong son for this favor. "Like I said, I haven't been a cop for a while. Sawyer or Atticus could—"

"Edward. Please." Her brown eyes darkened with her plea.

A muscle twitched beneath the scar on his jaw. He'd barely gotten himself to the cemetery. He'd already agreed to talking some cautionary sense into his brothers. He wasn't equipped to ask questions or search for clues or go anywhere near a police investigation—not when the consequences for getting involved were so high.

"I can't have the man I love anymore. But he was truly one of Kansas City's finest for thirty-six years. He left the military and became a police officer the year I found out I was pregnant with you. That badge represents the best years of our lives together. All that he did for this city, the man he was, the sons we raised. It represents so much more than just his job to me. Does that make any sense?"

He'd packed away everything that represented his wife and child when he'd lost them. But one thing he'd taken to heart from those first few sessions with his trauma counselor—every person grieved in his or her own way. While he wanted to erase every painful reminder of loss from his life, his mother wanted to cling to the memories. Edward understood what she was asking of him. He understood that he was asking it of himself as well, though he couldn't be sure how he was going to make it happen, or when, or what it might cost him.

"I want your father's badge. If it takes two days or two years or forever to track it down, I want it back."

"Okay." That single word hurt—down deep in his soul. Even though this assignment was an unofficial one, he was going to be a cop again.

"Okay? You'll do that for me?"

Edward wasn't in any kind of shape to be making promises to anybody. But he made this one to his mother.

"I'll do it."

Chapter Two

December

With eight months of hard-fought sobriety inside him to filter his thoughts, Edward managed to keep a wiseacre response to himself as the teen with the bright smile behind the cash register chirped, "Merry Christmas!" and handed him his bags of groceries.

"Thank you for shopping with us, sir," the girl went on, either genuinely caught up in the goodwill of the season or intent in her desire to impress her supervisor. Said supervisor, sporting a bit more weariness to his frozen smile, was pacing the bustling check-out lines, ensuring every customer had a positive shopping experience and would return to buy holiday turkeys and hams and whatever last-minute presents they might need in the upcoming two weeks.

At the girl's tender age, Edward suspected it was the former. He tucked his billfold into the back pocket of his jeans and unhooked his cane from the edge of the counter before grabbing the two plastic bags. He sincerely hoped the young cashier would be way past his thirty-five years of age before learning to hate the cheer and dazzle and social expectations of the holidays as much as he did.

The economy might thrive on the holiday season. A few Pollyannas might. But Edward Kincaid did not.

For him, Christmas meant violence and loss and a lifetime of happiness and purpose he might never find again.

"Merry Christmas, sir." The supervisor's greeting echoed the cashier's as Edward limped past.

His memory played a sweet lispy voice inside his head. *"Merry Christmas, Daddy. Did you get my bike?"*

"I did. A purple one. Merry Christmas, baby."

He blinked, as if a physical jerk could shut off the nightmare of those last few moments of his daughter's life. If he never said those words again, it would be too soon.

Clamping down on the bile of regret that rose in his throat, Edward acknowledged the man with a nod and walked out the sliding door, turning his face to the biting wind of a Missouri winter. He relished the icy crystals in the air, stinging his face and neck. Winter had come early to Kansas City this year. Snow had been on the ground for three weeks now, long enough to pack into drifts against buildings and trees and for grading salt and traffic to coat the pavement with a slick, slushy glop. The moisture beading on his charcoal sweater and the unzipped black coat he wore indicated another layer of this snowy mess was on the way. The dropping temperature that seemed to settle in his mended joints confirmed it.

Edward plunged the tip of his cane into the slush beside the curb, feeling even that tiny step down like the jab of a pin in his right ankle and knee. The twinges in his rebuilt body were tolerable most days. According to the doctors who'd stitched him back together, he was as healed as he was going to get. Now it was just a matter of building strength and continuing with his physical therapy exercises to maintain flexibility. His youngest brother, Holden, had insisted on giving him his weight-training set when he'd upgraded to newer equipment. Months of PT had made Edward fit. Dragging himself to the weight bench every time the need for a drink tried to take hold was getting him back into fighting shape. With the idea in mind that he'd wind up an arthritic old man before his time if he didn't keep moving, Edward stretched his legs out to lengthen his stride and crossed the parking lot to his black SUV.

He'd just tossed the grocery sacks into the back seat of the Grand Cherokee when the cell phone on his belt hummed with an incoming call. He climbed in behind the wheel, tossed his cane over to the passenger side and started the vehicle's powerful engine before unclipping the phone and checking the number. It was his youngest brother, Holden.

Edward cranked the defroster and opened the phone with a grin. "What do you want?"

"Bah, humbug to you, too." Holden's deep-pitched voice was laced with equal parts teasing and reprimand. "Where are you?"

Watching the first crystalline flakes dot his windshield and then melt away, Edward arched a dark brow with knowing sarcasm. Baby Bro wanted something. "I'm sitting in the grocery store parking lot, trying to get comfortable in my new car. You know, I had my old Jeep all broken in before you borrowed it and returned it a totaled mess after your jaunt down to the Ozarks with your girlfriend. This new model the insurance paid for doesn't feel like home yet. It still has that new upholstery smell."

"Um, hello? Witness protection? Bullets flying? You're lucky *I* didn't come back totaled."

Damn lucky. Despite Holden's sharpshooter and survival training with KCPD's S.W.A.T. team—and the loan of Edward's vehicle and expertise in hiding out from the world—he'd barely managed to stay a step ahead of the assassin who'd targeted the woman who'd witnessed their father's murder. Liza Parrish would probably be dead right now if Holden hadn't stepped up to volunteer as her personal bodyguard. Along with Sawyer's discovery of a dangerous conspiracy, and evidence that provided motive and a list of suspects that Atticus had uncovered, Liza's testimony had given KCPD a good description of their father's murderer or murderers.

Eight months had passed since John Kincaid's beaten body had been found slain, execution-style, in an abandoned riverfront warehouse. Edward's years of experience on the force warned him that the longer it took to solve the case, the harder it would be to find the answers they needed. But soon, very soon, KCPD would put someone behind bars for the vicious crime and justice would finally be served.

If the Kincaid brothers had anything to do with it.

Three of them, at any rate. He was willing enough to help out where he could, but it had been a long time since Edward had picked up his gun and badge. If he could remain on the sidelines, it was probably just as well. His last few days as a full-fledged cop hadn't done the people he cared about any good.

Pushing aside a niggling thought that was part relief, part regret and all guilt, Edward turned his focus back to his brother's call. "I guess I'd rather have you around instead of that old Jeep."

"You sweet talker, you."

Right. *I love you* came about as easily to his lips as *Merry Christmas*. Holden understood.

"So, what's up?" Edward asked, noting how the

snow gathering in the clouds above had turned the afternoon into a hazy twilight.

"I want you to come to Christmas Eve dinner at Mom's house."

Little Brother didn't beat around the bush, did he.

Though the idea of a family get-together, with presents and ornaments and food and laughter and love, hit him like a blinding sucker punch, Edward buried his knee-jerk reaction beneath the sarcasm that laced his voice. "I'm busy on the twenty-fourth."

"Bull—"

"Watch your mouth, little brother."

"When are you going to move on, Edward?" Holden asked, managing to sound irritated and concerned at the same time.

"I'm working on it." Edward idly looked out the window to see people hunched down in their coats and scarves against the weather, their arms laden with sacks and packages, purses and briefcases—all going somewhere with a purpose. He used to be driven like that. Catch some bad guys, save the day. Hurry home to make love to his wife and play kickball or tag or read a book with his daughter. Since their deaths, it had taken him four months to get out of the hospital and learn to walk again, the rest of the year to move out of his house to a cabin in the countryside outside of K.C.—to settle in a quiet place where the memories couldn't find him. It had taken longer still before a visit from his family or a trip to the store didn't drain every last ounce of his emotional energy. "I'm working on it," he repeated.

"I know you've come a long way. But…please. This will be Mom's first Christmas without Dad. I think we should all be there for her. I think we all need to be together."

So, when did the youngest of Edward's brothers start to sound like the wise old man of the family?

"I don't want to ruin anyone's holiday with one of my moods." He groused a curse beneath his breath. "Staying away might be the best gift I could give Mom."

"Nobody believes that but you, big brother." Holden's voice brightened, changing the tone if not the topic. "We'd love it if you'd come, even if it's just for a little while. Liza and I have an announcement to make."

"Surprise, surprise. Are you finally gonna make an honest woman of her?"

"Finally? Give me a break, Dr. Romance. I was in the hospital recovering from a sucking chest wound and a concussion after our run-in with Z Group's assassin, Mr. Smith." Holden's news didn't surprise him. With a hit man relentlessly trying to silence Liza's testimony about their father's murder, falling in love had happened fast. But even Edward's cynical soul had been able to see the depth of what was between them. "Then we had to find a new place for Liza that had room for three dogs after her house got all shot up. Those are all legitimate excuses for delaying wedding plans with the woman you love."

"Got that out of an etiquette book, did you?"

But Holden wouldn't be dissuaded. "So, are you coming to Mom's or not?"

"She knows I love her." He deserved a little flak for dropping out of the family—out of life—for so long. But he was making an effort—improving his family relationships, day by day. The rest of the world would have to wait to get his charming self back into the thick of things. "I'm a lot better about calling her than I was even a few months ago. Talked to her last night, in fact. I know she's planning a quiet family kind of thing—Sawyer with his wife and son and mother-in-law, Atticus and Brooke with her aunts, you and Liza, Uncle Bill."

"You're on the guest list, too. Even if you're just there for a…"

For a what? Edward whistled a long breath between his lips, feeling, not for the first time, the pain his addiction had cost his family. "A toast?"

"Sawyer's wife, Mel, is pregnant, so she won't be drinking any alcohol, either. Maybe none of us will. You know how Mom likes that sparkling cider."

"Relax, little brother. Mentioning booze is not going to make me go out and have a drink." There were a dozen other things that might tempt him to go back inside the store for a six-pack, but the mere mention of alcohol wasn't one of them. "I'm okay. I'll…think about the Christmas Eve thing."

"You've already decided not to come, haven't you."

"Maybe I can stop by on another day." And he *would* make the effort to do so. It was one thing for him to suffer through the season, but now that he was sober, he knew there was no good reason for his family to hurt any more than they had to. "Congratulations to you and Liza, though. I promise not to tell anyone until you make a formal announcement."

"I've got eight days to change your mind. I'm not giving up."

"Didn't think you would." The interior of the new Jeep had warmed up enough that Edward tucked the phone between his shoulder and ear and pulled off his black leather gloves. "Now, do you have some other reason for calling besides pestering me about family reunions?"

"I might."

"Come on. I've been sitting here long enough that it's snowing again. So spit it out."

Though he normally went out on calls with his S.W.A.T. team, Holden had been assigned to temporary light duty—aka sitting behind a desk—since going back to work at the Fourth Precinct after his hospital stay and recovery time. Edward could hear some papers rustling in the background as Holden's voice dropped to barely more than a whisper. "We've come up with a lead on Dad's murder that we—Sawyer, Atticus, Kevin Grove—the lead detective on the case—and me—believe we need *your* help to follow up on."

"Me? I've got until January second to let Major Taylor know whether or not I'm coming back to KCPD. Until then, I'm off duty. I don't even carry my badge anymore."

"Exactly. You may have street connections that we could use beyond the standard pawn shops and fences."

Edward had worked overt and undercover drug enforcement for most of his KCPD career. Once he'd had connections on both sides of the law. But since plowing André Butler beneath the wheels of his SUV, Edward hadn't gone near any of his old "friends." "You want me to do something illegal? Conduct a search without an official warrant?"

"All I want is for you to help us look for a ring. And maybe a couple of disintegrating bullets."

"DASHING THROUGH THE SNOW…"

Holly Masterson's singing softened to a hum as she squinted at her computer screen and typed in the next line of her autopsy report. *COD—Natural Causes. Massive heart failure due to…*

"In a one-horse open sleigh…"

Her fingers danced over the keyboard in time to

the music playing over her earphones. *Indigent lifestyle of malnutrition, exposure to elements and lack of medical...*

"...laughing all the way. Ha, ha, ha. Bells on—"

The red light flashed on her office phone, indicating an incoming call. Holly killed the music as she saved her report. She spared a few moments to back it up to a disk and send it to the printer before pulling off her earphones and answering the call. "Crime lab. Dr. Masterson speaking."

"Do I really have to call you *Doctor?* Can't I just call you Squirt, the way I used to?" Holly grinned at the teasing in her older brother Eli's voice. "So,what's keeping you at the lab so late tonight? I tried to call you on your cell, but it went straight to voice mail."

After a half dozen calls from the same unnamed cell phone, with no one on the other end when she picked it up, Holly had turned hers off and plugged it into its charger. But she had helped Eli raise herself and their younger sister since she was in high school and their parents had died in a plane crash. They'd weathered their sister's rebellious choices and cocaine addiction together. A wrong number was nothing to worry an overprotective big brother about.

"I like to call it 'work'," Holly deadpanned. "You know I man the late shift at the lab, or you wouldn't be calling me this close to midnight. So what's up?"

"A guy can't call his sister just to see how she's doing?" That dry wit was a Masterson trait. "So… your car's running all right? You got the stopper on that bathroom drain fixed? You're not dating anyone I need to check out?"

"Yes. I'll get to it. And no." Holly grinned. "So, what's going on that's so important you needed to stay up past your bedtime and chat before our regular Friday lunch?"

Several minutes later, Holly was pacing in front of the windows that separated her office from the darkened lab and the autopsy room beyond. This close to the holidays, the crime lab ran a skeleton crew at night. Other than the derelict John Doe lying in the morgue, Holly was alone in the basement. She knew lab techs on the floors above her were monitoring ongoing fiber trace tests and editing background noise off some security camera footage. And she was having one of her own team members rerun a ballistics test on what she'd dubbed a disintegrating bullet—a mysterious new design of deadly ammunition that had shown up in several autopsies this year. Unfortunately, even by the time she'd discovered them inside the murder victims, the bullets had already begun to decompose, making it impossible to read striations and trace them back to the gun that fired it. They'd be lucky if her ballistics specialist, Rick Temple, could determine the manufacturer and caliber of the bullet.

But that was all backlog work. Without any pressing case demands, Holly herself had been making the most of the relatively quiet night—destressing with some music and reading through hard copies of reports. Ever since a virus introduced by an offsite hacker had destroyed several computer records back in April, she'd been using slow nights like this one to rebuild files and rerun tests where there was still evidence available. She took pride in her team's clean chain-of-evidence record, and it galled her to think that one happy hacker could throw a monkey wrench into what had previously been solid cases, forcing investigations to be delayed or even circumstantial corroboration to be tossed out of ongoing trials. It was a matter of professional pride for Holly to make those evidence reports right again. For the victims in those cases, it was a matter of justice.

But with Eli's phone call, a much more personal stress had returned. She'd find a way to handle this one, too. Raking her fingers through her short, dark hair, she repeated her argument to her brother.

"Jillian will be just fine. She came out of rehab a lot stronger than either of us expected, so you know that hardheaded Masterson gene is in her somewhere." Eli had been worried about his other sister, not her, after all. "There's no need for you and Shauna to cancel your holiday cruise. Between your job with the D.A.'s office and her responsibilities running KCPD, you two have never even had a honeymoon. And you've been married almost two years. Go. Have a merry Christmas. Not having to worry about our little sister is my gift to you."

But Eli wasn't convinced. "It's not Jillian who concerns me. If that Blake Rivers bastard is back in town, then you know he's going to put pressure on her to get back together with him. I swear to God, Holl, after all those years with the drugs when we thought we might lose her, Jillian is finally on a healthy, positive track. She's gone back to college. She's volunteering with those kids at the youth center. If getting back with her old spoiled, party-time boyfriend knocks her off her game again…"

"You'll do what? You know, just because you're not a cop anymore doesn't mean you don't have to follow the rules."

"I didn't follow them when I *was* a cop."

Holly tucked her long bangs behind one ear, nodding her head in wry agreement. Following the rules was one Masterson trait that was uniquely hers. "We have to give Jillian the chance to make her own decisions and then stand up to the consequences on her own. We can't bulldoze in and take care of everything for her. That'd just be a form of co-dependency all over again."

The flicker of a shadow moved past the translucent glass door leading to the hallway, interrupting her thoughts and pacing. She *was* alone down here, wasn't she? That's why she'd dimmed the lights outside her office. No sense wasting the energy if she was the only one working in the lab. John Doe certainly didn't need the light.

She stared hard at the clouded glass, waiting for the movement in the hallway to repeat itself. She wasn't one to doubt what she'd seen, but she did like to have an explanation for things—be it an overnight cleaning staff employee coming in early, an electric short in one of the hallway lights, or even something as arcane as a ghost. She just wanted to know.

The glass darkened for an instant as the shadow passed by in the opposite direction.

"Holly?"

Jumping inside her skin at the prompt of Eli's voice, she turned away from the distraction and focused on making her point. "You and Shauna need to get on that plane tomorrow and fly to Florida. Take your cruise. Enjoy it. Jillian needs to be the one to tell Blake where to get off if he tries to rekindle a relationship she's not interested in."

"What if she *is* interested? What if Rivers won't take no for an answer? I'll be a thousand miles away."

"You'll be right where you should be. With your wife." Holly circled around behind her desk, double-checking the duty log and silently accounting for all the staff and techs scheduled to be in the building at this hour. "I can look out for Jillian. And I'll handle Blake, too, if he causes trouble."

"I always could count on you to be the sensible one." Some of the tension eased from Eli's voice and she could imagine him smiling. "All right. I'll go. I'll have my phone, though. If you need anything, call me."

"No. I won't. If something comes up, I'll take care of it myself." With one part of her brain still marking off people she'd seen in their labs, offices or the break room, Holly tried to put her brother completely at ease. He had a honeymoon to get to, after all. "I appreciate your concern, but I'm a big girl. So is Jillian. The two of us have already planned to have Christmas dinner and exchange gifts. We'll be fine. Have a wonderful trip. Put on some sunscreen and give my love to Shauna."

Eli hesitated for a moment, but ultimately, he gave in. "You're sure?"

"Positive."

"All right. I'll do my best to enjoy some quality time alone with my gorgeous wife." Holly smiled as she was meant to and he continued, "Love you, sis."

Though she suspected he'd leave his phone on 24/7—just in case—he conceded that at thirty-five, with a doctor's degree and a demanding job, she was a big enough girl to handle herself and their sister's ex-boyfriend if need be. "Love you, too, Eli. Bon voyage."

After hanging up, Holly checked the clock on the wall in her office. A few minutes past midnight. Time to shut things down and head out.

But though she turned off her computer and locked up the hard copies of the files she'd had out, Holly Masterson wasn't about to leave her lab until the mystery of the out-of-place shadow was resolved. She turned on her cell phone in case Jillian called and dropped it into her lab coat pocket. After closing the office door behind her, she flipped on the lights and ventured out into the bright, chilly sterility of the lab. Pausing only to turn off the colored lights on the miniature artificial Christmas tree she'd set on one of the stainless steel counters, she made a quick circle around the empty room, peeked in on John Doe in his drawer, then headed for the hallway door.

There, she turned off all the interior lights again and waited. If there was a short in one of the hall sconces that was going on and off and creating the illusion of shadows, it would be easy to spot from this vantage point. *Wait for it. Wait for it.* "Hmm. No problem with the lights."

Checking that possibility off her list, she opened the door a crack and listened for sounds. No ding of the elevator's bell, no whir of it rising on its cables and pulleys. No footsteps. Nothing beyond the endless whoosh from the heating vents, trying to warm up the common areas of the building to a more humane environment than the cooler temps used in the labs. So she *was* alone. Unwilling to give much credence to the ghost theory, Holly deduced that someone had walked past the door—twice—while she'd been on the phone with Eli. Someone who was lost because her lab, office and the autopsy room were the only destinations on this level. Yet no one had come in. Asked for directions. Shown up to ID the body in her morgue. So, who would be wandering through the basement at this time of night?

No one, apparently. It was probably the late hour that had her spooked. "Give it a rest, girl."

Ignoring the twinge of annoyance that she couldn't solve a simple mystery, Holly pulled the door shut behind her and jogged up the stairs to the first floor. The stairwell proved empty as well, and since she hadn't heard the elevator moving, there was no sense looking there. She nodded to the guard manning the reception desk on her way to the locker rooms at the rear of the building. But the need to find an answer just wouldn't go away.

Holly fisted her hands inside the pockets of her white coat and turned back to the guard. "Floyd? Did you see anyone going down to the basement? Within the last ten minutes or so?"

He looked up from the paper he was reading. "No, ma'am. No one's been in or out the lobby for the past hour. The cleaning crew's not set to come until one."

"None of the guards were making rounds downstairs, were they?"

"Not that I know of. Is there a problem, Doctor?"

Holly shook her head and smiled. "I thought I saw someone down there, but no one checked in with me at my office."

Floyd reached for his cap. "Would you like me to run down and sweep for an intruder?"

"No, no." She waved him back to his seat. "There are only so many ways to get in or out of the basement, and if you didn't see anyone on the elevator or the stairs…?"

He wrinkled up his forehead with an apology. "Not for the past hour, ma'am. Not until you came out that door just now."

"Okay. Well, maybe I just imagined the company." She didn't quite believe that, but without any evidence or witnesses to the contrary, there was nothing to do but go home. "Good night, Floyd. I'll see you tomorrow."

"Good night, ma'am."

Once inside the locker room, Holly shed her lab coat and hung it inside her locker. Since she'd already traded her surgical blues for warm jeans and a turtleneck sweater after completing John Doe's autopsy, changing for the drive home only meant bundling up for the winter weather outside.

Pushing aside the gun and holster she wore on field calls, Holly pulled her teal-green stocking cap and matching scarf from the top shelf.

Once she had her coat buttoned up, she turned on the blinking red nose of the Rudolph pin at her lapel. The gaudy reindeer jewelry was a testament to her late mother, who'd loved to decorate and celebrate the holidays in a big way. Her parents had been gone for fifteen years, her family fractured. But over the years, she'd grown closer to Eli and Jillian than they'd ever been as children. Now, instead of missing her parents, she paid homage to them by maintaining some of their happiest—and goofiest— traditions. Touching the pin and feeling a loving smile from somewhere in Heaven, Holly grabbed her purse and gloves and headed for the exit.

If she was lucky, the streets would be cleared, the traffic would be light and she could get home to her apartment and get some decent sleep before she had to report for work again in the morning.

She had just pulled one glove on when her cell phone rang. Surely Eli wasn't calling for another round of how she and Jillian couldn't survive without big brother in the house. Reaching into her purse, she pulled out her phone. The same familiar word instead of a number stared back at her.

Unnamed.

"Okay, fella." Breathing out a weary sigh, Holly opened the phone. "Hello?"

Nothing. But the connection was live. She could hear the faint hiss of shallow breathing in the background.

"Hey. I know you're there. You have the wrong number. You need to stop calling me." More silence. Not even so much as a suggestive or crude message if that was his intent. Just…someone listening. "Who is this?"

Click.

She jerked the phone from her ear as if the soft disconnect had been a zap of static electricity.

What the hell kind of psych game was this? Holly snapped the phone shut and dropped it into her purse as she pushed open the door to the main hallway. "Idiot."

A blur of white lunged at her from around the corner. "Gotcha!"

Holly yelped, automatically punching at the man who'd startled her while her heart was already thumping in her chest. "Damn it, Rick!"

Guffaws of deep-pitched laughter faded into a wide toothy grin on Rick Temple's clean-shaven face. "Oh, that one was priceless. If you could see your expression." He rubbed at a spot on his shoulder. "But you've got a mean punch, Doc."

Talk about idiots. How one man could know so much about forensic science and yet beans about interacting with people in a mature, normal way eluded her. "What are you, in junior high? Sorry about the bruise, but startling the crap out of me is not funny."

"Depends on your perspective."

Holly flashed a grin that was more of a sneer than sincere. "You're a grown man. One of these days you're going to have to start acting like one. These practical jokes are hard on my blood pressure."

"Oh, but you make it too easy, lady. Walking around all serious, focused all the time. I've got to lighten you up."

"Giving me gray hairs isn't the kind of lightness I find amusing."

"You're not that old, Doc. You've got to start having some fun." At least he had the decency to retrieve the glove she'd dropped. She knew him to be thirty-two years old, but the grin he still wore looked two decades younger as he handed over the glove. "Think of these little encounters as my way of keeping you on your toes."

Did he think she wasn't doing her job? The corrupted evidence files she'd been trying to re-create made her prickle a little more defensively than usual. Not for the first time, she wondered how much of Rick's teasing was really a warped sense of humor and how much might be resentment that *she'd* gotten the supervisory job that they'd both applied for. It might be wise for her to remind him who was in charge. "You know, Rick, if you weren't

as good at your job as you are, I might have to write
you up for your… personality quirks. If any of your
jokes interfere with anyone's ability to do their
job…"

"Oh, good one, Doc. Flatter me and call me out,
all in the same sentence." He pulled back the front of
his lab coat and shoved his fingers into the front
pockets of his jeans. "I just wanted to catch you
before you left and let you know that the preliminary
report on that bullet I'm processing doesn't look
promising. I've been able to break it down into its
components, and maybe even tell you how they're
decomposing so quickly. But pull a manufacturer's
name off it? Even at a microscopic level, I haven't
been able to pull anything substantive off the casing."

Good. Fortunately, he could be serious when he
talked about work. "Any luck with the caliber?"

"I'm guessing a thirty-five mil. I should be able
to give you something definitive by the morning."

Holly was breathing normally now. Her smile
was genuine. And another possibility regarding the
mysterious shadow had presented itself. "Thanks,
Rick. Say, were you down in the basement a few
minutes ago, trying to catch me with your update?
I was on the phone, but you could have come in."

"No." As her humor returned, his faded. "I just
now came down from the ballistics lab. Are you
checking on me every moment of every shift now?
Or do you just miss working side by side with me?"

"We still have plenty of opportunities to work together. I thought someone might be looking for me, that's all. Thanks. I'll look forward to that full report."

"First thing in the morning, I promise. You headed out?"

She nodded. "I'm done for the night. See you at seven?"

"I'll be here."

"Good night."

"Boo." He flashed his hands in her face, startling her slightly. "Too easy. Just too damn easy." Rick's chuckle disappeared with him into the men's locker room.

Shaking her head, Holly pulled on her remaining glove and turned toward the exit to the parking garage.

Nine nights out of ten, Holly enjoyed working the late shift. With a few juvenile colleague exceptions, she preferred the quiet and solitude of the nighttime hours. Dealing with fewer people meant she could concentrate on her work. Dissecting bodies and processing biological evidence tended to have an isolating effect in the first place, but the calm and quiet and focus on the job were what allowed her to deal with crime scenes that could often be gruesome, and victims who were always some form of tragic. Having to deal with the victim's family or witnesses on top of the crime itself could be draining.

Yet tonight she couldn't seem to settle inside her skin.

Holly pushed open the thick steel door that led from the lab building into the attached parking garage. The heels of her boots grated against the concrete as she strode to her car, the abrasive grinding of soles and grit echoing off the walls of the garage. There was an edginess crawling through her veins, and despite knowing she'd be reporting to help with a double-shift in the morning, she was beginning to think she wasn't going to be getting much sleep tonight.

She didn't know if it was the unexplained shadow or the pesky anonymous phone calls that had her so off-kilter. Maybe it was Rick's eternal pleasure at getting a rise out of her or the conversation she'd had with Eli. No doubt it was a combination of all those things that made her so uneasy.

Lengthening her stride, she hurried past cars and trucks and empty parking slots. She pulled her keys from her purse and squeezed her fist tighter around the shoulder strap. Chances were, she was subconsciously preparing herself for another surprise from Rick.

That's why, when she heard a car door open, she didn't immediately panic. Enough was enough. If he wanted to keep playing these games, then she would chew him up one side and down the other like the immature child he was.

Only, that was no child climbing out of the black Jeep next to her Honda. And it wasn't Rick.

Holly stopped. Stared. Retreated a step as a

dark-haired man slowly unfolded himself from behind the wheel.

Rick Temple was merely annoying. *This* guy made her curl her toes inside her socks and brace for trouble.

When she wore her high-heeled boots, Holly stood six feet tall. This guy was taller. Broader. The brass tip of a cane clacked against the concrete, drawing her attention down to the ground for a split second. When the car door closed, her gaze darted back up to collide with eyes that were gray and hooded and cold like steel. The late-night shadow of his beard was scraggly and dark and added an air of menace to his square jaw and angular features. Despite the cane, he moved from the shadows with a deliberate grace and Holly instinctively backed away.

"Dr. Masterson?" His gritty voice was deep in pitch, but hoarse, as though a cold had settled in his throat.

He knew her name? "Yes?"

Was that her pulse hammering in her ears? Or warning drums thundering inside her head?

The gray eyes cut right to the truth. "Don't be afraid of me."

Impossible.

"I need to talk to you."

This man was no shadow.

And he was no practical joke.

Chapter Three

Great job, Lieutenant. The woman was running.

"Dr. Masterson?"

In the time it took her to spin around and move those long legs a couple of steps, Edward hooked his cane around her elbow. She twisted to escape but he tugged her off balance and caught her with his hand.

"Let go of me!"

When her leather purse came sailing toward his head like a roundhouse punch, he deflected the blow with his shoulder. "Hey! Watch it!"

A knee came next. He was forced to drop his cane and wrap both hands around her upper arms to protect himself.

"Let. Go," she said through gritted teeth.

"You don't understand." There wasn't much meat on her tall, lean figure, but what was there was all muscle. As his grip tightened, her struggles increased. "I just want to talk."

"Then let go."

"You'll run."

"I'll scream."

She was already making plenty of noise. Edward stifled a sigh. Their names had crossed during one investigation or another. He recognized her face from trials where they'd both testified. But he was still a virtual stranger. He should have introduced himself. Man, was he out of practice in dealing with people.

Trying to look less threatening and guessing he was failing miserably, Edward guided her back against a concrete pillar, easing his grip on the pink wool of her coat. "I'm not going to hurt you. I'm a…" *Cop.* Wrong. He couldn't exactly say that anymore. "I'm Edward Kincaid. You know my brothers Sawyer and Atticus. You and I have met briefly before—a couple of years back. Through work." He waited for the names to register, the recognition to show in her eyes. Framed by long sable lashes, they were hazel green with beautiful gold sunbursts, doubts and suspicion shining from them. His hands were simply resting against her sleeves now, though he had her escape pretty well blocked with his body. "I need to ask you some questions about my father's murder."

She finally stopped twisting like a fish on the end of a hook, but her nostrils flared and her narrow chest rose and fell, unexpectedly distracting him, as she fought to regain control her breathing and this ridiculously out-of-whack meeting. "John Kincaid? You're his oldest son?"

"Yes."

"The late deputy commissioner was your father?"

"Yes. You performed his autopsy."

Her eyes narrowed past pretty and she batted his hands away. "Haven't you heard of the telephone?"

"I thought this was a conversation better done face-to-face." Raising his hands in mute surrender, he tried to show her—albeit a little too late—that he had no intention of harming her. "I didn't expect you to think you were being assaulted. I guess my face has changed more than I realized since the last time our paths crossed."

"You said that before. When did we work together?"

"We testified at the same trial." He shoved his hands into the pockets of his black leather coat. She didn't need to see the fists he had to make in order to say the dead man's name. "André Butler's."

"Yes, of course, I remember now. Drug trafficker. Gang leader. Fancied himself a mini mobster. That ended in a mistrial. He… Oh."

The color drained from her cheeks. He could see the apology—then the pity—cross her expression almost as quickly as the recognition appeared. She was checking out the scars along his jaw from the crash. Remembering the headlines. Maybe she'd even attended the funeral. The one that he'd been too busted up to remember much about. "I'm sorry. So sorry. Your family. I worked on all three…" She pressed her lips together, cutting that line of conversation. "Of course, I remember you. You should have introduced yourself sooner, Detective."

"Let's just go with Edward or Kincaid for now." He wasn't about to explain that one. He drew in a deep breath, determined to start this conversation all over again. If Holden could talk him into doing some legwork on this case, then he'd better do it right. His fists eased their grip inside his pockets. "I apologize for alarming you, but I was told you worked the night shift. I thought I could catch you on the way home."

"Instead, you scared the life out of me," she said. He turned to keep her in his line of sight as she moved away from the pillar to the open area in the middle of the garage. He'd give her the space and pray that with those legs she didn't bolt. In some ways, he was in better shape than he'd been before the accident. But he didn't think his right knee and ankle had a quick sprint left in them. "If you need to consult on a case, you should make an appointment."

Turn around. Look me in the eye. Show me you're not running. "This isn't exactly an official visit," he explained.

With that, she stopped. He forced himself to look away from the heart-shaped rounding of her bottom as she squatted down in her jeans. *Just being polite,* he told himself, pretending a few dormant male hormones hadn't just stirred to life below his belt buckle. Well, if feeling guilty at perking up over a woman who wasn't his late wife didn't put him in a mood, then Holly Masterson's actions did.

She stood and turned, holding out the cane she'd picked up. Held it out with an apologetic *"Sorry"* like he was some kind of crippled old man who needed her help.

Edward snatched it from her grasp and plunked the tip down on the concrete, feeling a sudden need to lean on its support.

"What is it, then?" she asked. Despite his surly lack of thanks, she was looking more curious than irritated now. And the fear he'd put in her eyes a few minutes ago was long gone. "Have you discovered a new lead on your father's murder?"

Right. He was here to work. To ask questions and do things a regular cop couldn't do. Hormonal reactions and hits to the ego had nothing to do with this. "Detective Grove is running the investigation, but I have a different angle I want to work on the case."

"And you have clearance to do that on your own father's murder?"

"I said it was unofficial."

"I see." She worked her green-gloved fingers around the strap of her shoulder bag. When the kneading movement stilled, she tipped her chin and looked him straight in the eye. "You do know that the two bullets I recovered from your father's body in April have since decomposed to the point that they're useless for any kind of clinical analysis. And that my lab's original ballistics and trace reports on them were purged from my computer files by a virus?"

His brothers had filled him in on the destruction of evidence that seemed too convenient to be any kind of accident. "Those are just a couple of the problems I have with this case. That's why I'm taking advantage of my…inactive…status with the department to do a little investigating on my own."

She clutched the strap tighter and took a step closer. "You think there's someone on the inside messing with this case?"

"Possibly." Somebody with connections somewhere had been systematically eliminating witnesses and destroying evidence almost as soon as they were uncovered. Z Group, the covert agency Edward and his brothers believed was behind their father's murder, had vast resources—enough to pay off or extort cooperation from almost anyone. It was the players who wouldn't cooperate—like John Kincaid—who'd been silenced. "I don't want to think it's a cop, but there are a lot of other people with connections to the department to consider as well— the lab, the press, technical staff, veterans, family."

She shook her head. "No one from my lab—"

"I'm not accusing you of anything. I'm just looking for answers."

Her smooth, unadorned lips curled into a pensive frown. But those hazel eyes indicated she'd been thinking something through from the moment he'd released her. It almost startled him when her face relaxed into a smile. "I've never liked an unfinished puzzle. As long as it's not illegal, how can I help?"

The steel door leading from the garage into the building opened behind her and a young man with spiky brown hair walked out. Edward lowered his voice. "I'd rather not discuss it here. Are you free right now? I'll buy you a cup of coffee."

It was half past midnight on a Wednesday morning. But he was hoping her work schedule meant she was a fellow night owl. "Well, I was planning to go home and get five hours of sleep before I have to turn around and come back to work in the morning. We're all covering extra shifts during the holidays so folks can go on vacation and be with their families."

Holidays. Holly. Oh, joy. The blinking reindeer nose on her coat had been far easier to ignore than the unique color of her eyes. But now Rudolph seemed to be flashing in his retinas like some kind of danger warning. Suddenly, what had just been another winter night was now one of the final shopping days left before Christmas. Suddenly, he was bleeding out in the snow and saying *Merry Christmas* to his daughter for the very last time.

"Hey."

Something soft and warm brushed across the back of his knuckles and Edward's eyes popped open. *Oh God.* Where had he gone? What had he said? Was he scowling as hard as the cramp in his jaw indicated? He needed to get out of here and get a beer.

No, Daddy. You promised.

"Fine. No beer."

"Excuse me?" The blurring of past and present cleared and he saw the green glove resting atop his hand where it fisted around his cane. He heard the articulate voice. Focused in on the confused concern shining in those clear green-gold eyes. "Are you okay?"

Every impulse in his body screamed to turn his hand and hold tight to Holly Masterson's gentle touch, as though it was a lifeline to sanity and redemption. But that was crazy. *He* was crazy. The good doctor was just being kind.

Edward wisely pulled away before she called the loony wagon on him. "Yeah. Um, sorry about that. I was asking—"

"Holly?" The young man who'd entered the garage a moment ago called to her from a pickup truck a couple of vehicles away. "Is everything okay? I thought you'd already gone."

Edward couldn't help but notice the flinch in her shoulders as the young man approached. *He'd* been looming over her like some kind of beast from a fairy tale, but this clean-cut college boy startled her?

"Sure, Rick. Everything's fine."

Rick's gaze darted from his coworker up to Edward and quickly back to Holly again. "Do you want me to wait for you to get into your car?"

"I said I was fine. Thanks for asking, though. I'll see you tomorrow." When she shifted her full attention back to his own beastly countenance, her voice was clear and certain. "Shall we go solve that puzzle? Edward?"

The man named Rick climbed into his truck and started the engine, but Edward was painfully aware that he didn't back out and drive away. He nodded to Holly, not sure if he was feeling ashamed or angered at the other man's assumption that, just by his fearsome appearance and proximity, he meant her harm. And why was it even more unsettling that her initial fear of him had abated to the point that it sounded as though she was defending him?

"Name the place," Edward answered, worried about just what kind of emotional roller coaster ride he'd signed up for when he'd agreed to help Holden find their father's killer. "I'll follow you."

He had a feeling the man named Rick would be following *him*.

THE MOONLIGHT CAFE AND COFFEE BAR on the Plaza stayed open until two in the morning between

Thanksgiving and New Year's to make the most of the influx of tourists and locals who came to see the million-plus holiday lights decorating nearly every rooftop line of the historic upscale shopping and entertainment district. Whether they'd come to have a drink, see a movie or soak up the pervasive holiday atmosphere, the sidewalks and streets were crowded. People from all over the city, and visitors staying in the nearby hotels, were walking about, looking in dressed-up storefront windows and enjoying the festive glow that was both literal and metaphoric this time of year.

The steady fall of light snow that added an extra few inches of white to the hilly streets didn't deter any of the couples sharing horse-drawn carriage rides. The dropping temperatures that nearly froze Brush Creek and the scenic walkway on either side of it didn't keep groups of young-somethings from taking souvenir pictures and hopping from one establishment to the next. If anything, the wintry weather seemed to intensify the laughter and "Look there!'s" and romantic appreciation for the district's Mediterranean architecture, statues and fountains, even if the water in the fountains had been turned off until spring.

Edward Kincaid, however, looked miserable.

Watching him across the polished black tabletop, Holly cradled a cup of almond green tea in her hands, warming her fingers and letting the aromatic steam waft through her nose and keep her senses energized. Edward had removed his leather coat to reveal that it wasn't shoulder pads that made him appear so broad and intimidating. His size and height were the real deal. The color of the heavy knit charcoal sweater he wore reflected in his gray eyes and made them equally dark.

He didn't smile, didn't say much beyond the business at hand, yet his eyes never seemed to be still. Though he continued to face Holly over his mug of black coffee, his gaze darted around, seeming to take in any nearby movement—the waitress carrying a tray, patrons settling in at the bar area, a couple packing up and leaving the booth behind Holly. He studied Holly herself, whenever she raised her cup to take a sip, or when she spoke.

There was something slightly unnerving about the intensity of his steel gaze, an alert watchfulness that made him seem inordinately aware of his surroundings. The man just couldn't seem to relax. Maybe it was a by-product of his time spent working as an undercover detective for KCPD's drug enforcement team. Or maybe he just didn't like the close confines of a crowd.

But to his credit, even when they had to wait ten minutes to get a table instead of sitting at the bar, he didn't complain. And though he hadn't zoned out on her again as though he was being buffeted by waves of pain, the way he had at the lab's parking garage, he didn't seem to say much more than he had to.

The brooding intensity and lengthy silences made Holly wonder just what was going on behind those alert, soulful eyes. Maybe because of the air of complexity that shrouded him, this secretive, solitary man definitely intrigued her.

"My apartment's not too far from here," she commented when she realized she was doing more studying than talking herself.

"One of the brownstones?"

Holly nodded. That's why she'd picked this particular place to share a conversation. While she knew *who* the detective sitting across from her was, she didn't really know him personally. And though she found Edward Kincaid the most interesting mystery to solve of the day, the practical experience of watching her younger sister allow one wrong man after another into her life—just to ensure her next fix—had taught Holly that acting impulsively on this strange attraction to the taciturn detective might not be the wisest move she could make. If things got too weird, she could quickly duck out and get home to the safety and serenity of her own place. "I live on one of the hills south of Brush Creek Boulevard, so I've got a great view of all the Christmas lights."

He didn't respond to that. After savoring a long drink from his mug, he shifted the conversation back to his reason for asking to meet her in the first place. "When you performed your autopsy on my father, was there any indication that he'd been wearing a ring?"

So much for getting acquainted. She'd already guessed that his raspy, low-pitched voice was a permanent thing—due to injury or surgery of some kind, not a temporary cold. And closer observation had shown her that his chocolate brown beard wasn't unkempt, after all. Instead, the scraggly effect was actually a normal midnight shadow coming in around a splash of scars that dotted his jawline and right cheek.

On the outside, she was learning about—and unexpectedly liking—Edward Kincaid. But no way was he going to let her see the man behind the eyes.

She reminded herself that this wasn't a date. He wanted to pick her brain about autopsies and corrupted lab reports.

"Let's see." Holly sipped her tea and sorted through the information inside her head. The kind of details he wanted had been deleted from her file by the virus, but she retained a mental image of every victim she'd ever worked on in her head and her heart. In her memory, she gently traveled over John Kincaid's bruised and broken body, stretched out beneath the bright lights of her lab. "He had a wedding ring on his left hand."

Edward sipped his coffee and nodded. "Mom

insisted he be buried with it. Could there have been a second ring?"

Her eyes closed and she drifted back in time to her lab. She tried to picture each hand in her mind. No indentations at the base of any finger, indicating the habitual wearing of any other jewelry. But a remembered notation popped into her head and she opened her eyes. "Wait." She set her cup in its saucer and leaned forward, gesturing across the back of her neck. "There was a long, thin abrasion at his nape. I thought it might be related to the beating he took. He'd been tied up so…"

A muscle ticked along his jaw as Edward pressed his lips into a thin grim line.

Holly instinctively reached across the table, cursing her own careless words. "I am so sorry." Just as quickly, she curled her fingers into her palm and drew them back. He was here for information, not sympathy. "It's a professional thing," she explained. "I have to stay clinical when I make these kinds of reports—so emotional reactions don't clog my perception of things—but I know it's personal for you. You don't want to hear—"

"I want to hear anything that can help." His words indicated that he'd learned to detach his emotions from his job as well. "Tell me about the mark on his neck."

For a moment, Holly was struck by the sheer strength of will it took to go through everything

Edward Kincaid had suffered and still be able to get up in the morning, much less carry on a conversation or run an investigation into something so personal, so violent. Maybe she'd just gotten her first glimpse inside the man.

And maybe she'd better shut off her speculation and any resulting compassion or admiration. He clearly didn't want to deal with his emotions. Holly took another sip of the tea that had grown tasteless on her tongue and continued. "I wish I could review my notes to be sure, but if I remember correctly, the mark was made postmortem. Something like that could be caused by tearing a necklace off someone's neck. Could your father have been wearing the ring on a chain?"

"It's possible. If the ring was something he'd had for a while, then it might not fit his fingers anymore. I never knew him to wear one. But then…" he leaned back against the black vinyl seat, "I dropped out of his life for a while." After losing his wife and daughter to a vengeful André Butler, that was probably an understatement. "I didn't even know he was looking into Z Group on his own time, so, why would I know about changes in the style of jewelry he wore?"

"Z Group? Your brother Atticus mentioned that when I was working a Jane Doe murder investigation with him. He thought she was connected to your father's murder—that they both had worked for the same security organization at one time. They were both killed with two shots—head and heart. Both with the same unique type of bullet."

Edward nodded. "Disintegrators. I'd love to get my hands on one—see if I can find anything that matches it on the underground market."

"I have a few samples in my lab. But the break-down rate is extreme once they enter the body and react with our biological chemicals." It amazed as much as sickened her to think that someone had created something that could be deadly one moment, then decompose beyond recognition the next. "You're welcome to come by and look at one, though I don't know how much good it would do you. I guess that's the point of making them in the first place—so someone can commit a crime and not leave a trail that can be traced."

"I intend to follow that trail all the way to the source." Edward's gaze zoomed in on hers. "I need you to understand something, Doctor."

Holly nearly had to hold her breath to keep from looking away from the piercing sensation of those eyes. "Okay?"

"If I have to break the law to do this, I am going to find out who killed my father."

There was no question that he meant every dramatic word. "You'd give up your badge?"

He braced his elbows on the table, steepled his fingers together at his scarred-up chin and leaned forward, eating up the space in the booth. "I don't know how much my badge is worth anymore since it got my wife and daughter killed. But I know what justice is worth." A chill of destiny—or maybe doom—washed over her, raising a sea of goose bumps across her skin. "If you don't want to help me, I understand. I don't want to jeopardize anyone's career but my own—not my brothers', not yours." Holly couldn't help it, she crossed her arms in front of her and tried to hug some warmth into her body. "But I owe this to my dad. I intend to do whatever it takes to put an end to Z Group and to prove who killed him."

It still stuck in Holly's craw that someone—most likely from Z Group—had hacked into her computer files and deleted key elements of reports relating to the murders of John Kincaid and others. She was always thorough, always precise. But now there were gaping holes in her work. Court orders, exhumation of bodies and second autopsies would allow her to replace most of that missing information—if the bodies hadn't degraded and embalming hadn't altered lingering evidence. But unless there was a new lead on a case, KCPD and the D.A.'s office hadn't been inclined to budget the expense or put the victims' families through any more pain or false hopes. She'd love the chance to make things right, to stamp a *Closed* on every corrupted investigation file. Reclaiming the accuracy of her work was a gut-deep need that could put

professional and personal frustrations and inse-
curities to rest.

But to skip protocols or break the law to find her
own satisfaction or personal vindication?

"Are you asking me to do something illegal for
you?"

His steely eyes didn't blink. "I'm asking you to
turn the other way if *I* have to."

Then this meeting was over. Holly began to slip
into her coat and gather her things. "What kind of
cop are you?"

No longer pretending that this had been some
kind of consultation between KCPD and the crime
lab, Edward pulled some bills from his wallet and
tossed them onto the table. "My father's badge was
never recovered from the kidnapping or murder
sites. Let's just say getting that badge back is more
important than keeping my own."

Holly shook her head before pulling her
stocking cap on over her hair. After living with the
uncertain future of being orphaned in college and
the frightening second-guessing and guilt of
raising a sister with a drug addiction, she
demanded honesty and dependability in her
world. Her science was safe—there were answers
and rules. She couldn't risk the hard-won security
of her life. Not even to solve a difficult case. Not
even if the man asking her to break the rules had
already touched something feminine and com-

passionate inside her. "It's late. I'd better be getting home."

"I'll walk you to your car."

Holly slid out of the booth to button her coat. "That's all right. I can take care of myself. Thanks for the tea."

Then she realized it had been a statement of fact, not a polite offer. Edward Kincaid moved surprisingly fast for a man who used a cane. Before she could wrap her scarf around her neck and grab her purse, he was out of the booth beside her, shrugging into his coat. "My father taught me to always walk a lady to her car this time of night."

No sense endangering herself, just to make a point. "All right. Thank you."

The guiding touch of his hand at the small of her back was warmer than the layers of wool and cotton she wore. The unexpected warmth was almost as unsettling as the bite of wind that hit her face when she pushed open the door.

His touch shifted but remained as Edward positioned himself to take the brunt of the wind. Like so many other couples around them, they strolled the wide sidewalks toward her car a couple of blocks away. The setting was festive and romantic, with the brightly colored lights overhead and swirling gusts of snow at their feet.

But there was nothing romantic about their conversation. "I don't want to deny you access to information that can help you find your father's killer."

"I appreciate that. Atticus and Sawyer said you'd been helpful in their investigations, so I thought you'd be the best place to start looking for answers."

Holly hunched her shoulders against the cold, wondering if she should shorten her stride to accommodate the slight limp in his right leg. But, as before, he didn't complain, didn't lag behind, and, when she snuck a sideways glance toward the grizzled line of his jaw, she saw that he wasn't grimacing in any kind of pain. So she just kept walking. He kept his hand at her back.

And scanned the street from side to side, marking each face as they passed, peeking into alleyways and between parked cars.

"Are you looking for someone?"

"Old habit." He nodded toward a vehicle about half a block away. "You're the silver Honda, right."

"Right." Old habit? As in, this hyperwatchfulness, ingrained from his time spent working undercover, was just a part of his everyday life now? Or was there something specific that had put him on guard tonight? Holly found herself paying a little more attention to the other people around them. "Believe me, I'd love to see your father's case put to rest and someone on trial for the crime. By all accounts, John was a good man—a well-respected leader in the department."

"He was."

Holly stopped beside her car and turned in front of him, putting up a warning hand. "But just so we're clear. If I find anything missing from my lab, any file copied, any evidence corrupted, I *will* report you."

"Skinny as a stick but you pack a punch." Was that a hint of a smile on his lips? His idea of a compliment? And when had he been sizing up her figure?

Probably the same time she'd been sizing up his.

"KCPD hasn't had a lot of luck going by the book on Dad's case." He switched the cane to his left hand and held up his right. "I promise to do everything I can by the rules—and I'll take any help you can give me. But mark my words—I'm prepared to do whatever it takes to bring in his killer."

"Anything?" she asked. "As is legal or not?"

"Anything."

Fine. So no guarantees from this man. *Tuck your fascination away. Put your curiosity aside. Keep everything strictly business with Edward Kincaid. Say good-night.*

Holly extended her hand. "It's been a pleasure to meet you, Detective… Edward."

"No, it hasn't." But his black leather glove wrapped around her green woolen one, anyway, swallowing her handshake up in his grip.

"Yes, it…" *Pull away.* She didn't. "Well, it was

between the I-thought-you-were-going-to-attack-me-in-the-garage part and the breaking-the-law part. It *has* been an interesting night."

"Why, Dr. Masterson, I do believe you have a sense of humor."

Holly bristled. What was with the analysis of her ability to make or get a joke tonight? She released his hand and opened her purse to unclip her keys. "Come by the lab tomorrow if you want to see the bullet. But I'm not letting it—or you—out of my sight."

Her cell phone rang and everything inside Holly instantly tensed. It rang a second time, and she wondered if it was worth pulling it out to read the all-too-familiar number.

"You need to get that?"

"No, I…" She'd answered too quickly. "At this time of night?"

"Could be a call to a crime scene."

"I'm off duty."

"Family emergency?"

Jillian. What if it *was* her sister calling for advice—or rescue.

Holly's deep breath clouded the air between them. When it cleared, she saw patient expectation in his expression. He wouldn't walk away until she answered it now. On the fifth ring, she pulled the phone from her purse and looked at the number.

Unnamed.

Son of a… Why wouldn't he stop? Holly turned

almost completely around, taking note of each passerby with a phone to his ear. Was somebody getting a kick out of harassing her like this?

"Holly?"

Edward's deep, raspy voice demanded an explanation.

He wasn't getting one.

Shutting off her phone, she buried it deep inside her coat pocket and pretended the relentless wrong number hadn't spooked her. "I'll see if I can find a photograph of the Cyrillic *Z* tattoo I found on all the Z Group victims. If the ring you're looking for is some kind of souvenir from the time your father and the others worked together, then maybe it will give you an idea of what you're looking for. If I can't find a photo, I'll sketch you a picture of what I remember. I'll have it ready when you come to inspect the bullet."

"Do you have a photographic memory?"

"Not exactly." Leaving him on the sidewalk, she circled around her car to the driver's side door. "Just a pretty good eye for details. I'll call you when I have something. Do you have a card where I can reach you?"

"No."

"Well, just tell me and I can punch it in, then."

"You've already turned off your phone and put it away. You don't want whoever that was to call you again." Her car sat between them, and yet she felt as though he was right in her face, probing deep inside her with those eyes of his. "I have a pretty good eye for details, too. And something about that phone call rattled you."

Chapter Four

"This little scheme of yours has dragged on for far too long, and gotten more complicated than I ever agreed to."

The man in the hallway glared down at the woman standing in the open doorway of her hotel suite. He'd had one hell of a day and an even longer night, balancing lies and truths—carefully feigning ignorance while maintaining a vigilant watch over his current assignment. He'd been well trained for this kind of patient, precise work. But the stress gave him a headache and made him eager to rip something in two.

And she had the gall to stand there at two in the morning with those lush pink lips and a sexy pout, wearing a white diaphanous nothing that captured the brightness of the snow and city lights shining through the floor-to-ceiling window across the room. He was frustrated as anything and dead set on altering their long-standing agreement, and yet she managed to look cool and desirable and completely unmoved by the trials of his day.

"Hello to you, too," she purred with amusement. The woman stepped aside and welcomed him into her suite. She locked the door and reached up to remove his coat, pointing him to the tray of drinks on the coffee table while she knocked the snow off the collar and hung the coat in the closet. "You're later than I expected. Any problems?"

She was lucky he'd shown up at all. Hers wasn't the only number on his phone he could call. There were better women in this world he could have if he wanted, but a pact with this she-devil had sealed his fate. He should remind her that she'd be nothing—she'd be dead—without his help, and that she should be grateful he'd continued the charade for this long. Instead, he poured himself a bourbon and drank the entire glass without voicing his rebellious thoughts.

While he savored the fire burning down his throat, the woman walked up behind him, sliding her hands across his shoulders and tugging his suit jacket down his arms. "You really need to learn to relax, my dear." The gold ring she wore sparkled with the lights from outside as she plucked the glass from his hand and used the motion of setting it on the table to slip around to the front and remove his jacket.

Like that ring had any real meaning to her. Yet of

all the baubles and souvenirs in her trinket box, the gold signet ring was the memento she enjoyed the most.

She tossed the jacket on the sofa and came back to play with the buttons beneath his tie. "How many times have I told you I have everything under control? I've never failed yet on a mission, not even when my so-called friends double-crossed me." She smoothed her palms across the fine-weave cotton of his dress shirt, stroking the skin underneath. "Trust the plan. KCPD may know bits and pieces, but they'll never put it all together. We've covered our tracks too well. We'll adjust when and if we need to. But for now…" she cupped her palms over the rise of his pectoral muscles "…trust *me*."

The man lurched at the wicked massage that hardened his nipples and betrayed the power she had over him.

"Stop it." He seized her wrists and removed her hands from his body. "We need to talk."

She raised her gaze to his. "You didn't come here to talk at this hour. You need to vent." With her arms pinned, she simply moved her body closer to make her point. "And I've always known the best way to relieve your stress, haven't I?"

He squeezed his eyes shut and weathered his body's traitorous response to hers. He was a professional, he told himself, a successful man in his own right. He'd earned his rank and expected others to respect his authority.

But now this curvaceous hellion was calling the shots, and he was at her mercy. In more ways than one.

He bent his head to capture her mouth with his. "There have been too many sloppy killings these past months to cover up our mistakes. Fierro. Those three escaped convicts you hired. Former Z Group operatives. Mr. Smith."

"Not sloppy. Brilliant." She freed her hands and tugged at the knot of his tie. "One man kills another. Or the police takes one out. And then I eliminate any killer who isn't completely loyal. Every path leads to a dead end. Our enterprise here in Kansas City can't be traced back to us." The buttons of his shirt went next. "You're not thinking of being disloyal, are you, dear?"

"Of course not." He pushed the straps of her gown off her shoulders, determined to take control of the conversation *and* the seduction. "But now you want to target the crime lab? It feels like an awful lot of work to cover up our business together."

His complaining made her testy. She ripped open the front of his shirt and kissed his chest. "Would you rather I allowed KCPD to connect the two of us together? Would you like to stop smuggling goods and information out of the country? The market in eastern Europe and the Middle East is more profitable than ever."

But he demanded she hear him out. "Yes. But Z Group has always had a designated hit man to eliminate problems. Holden Kincaid shot Mr. Smith—our latest go-to man—dead. It's too risky to conduct business without a safety net like that." He picked her up and carried her through the doorway into the bedroom. "I want to cease operations for a while, allow KCPD's fixation with Z Group to die down. I've managed to stall out their investigation for now."

She laughed against his lips. "You're a fool to think anything will 'die down.' That's why we have to keep playing the game until we win. Those Kincaid boys are just like their father. You may have thrown up a few roadblocks to impede their investigation, but they won't give up until they have a murderer to put away. And since Irina Zorinsky Hansford is already dead…"

"Enough, woman! That's what I'm talking about." He set her down and shoved her away, breaking the seductive contact so he could think straight. He raked his fingers through his hair. "Irina's *death* thirty years ago is what started this whole mess. When she was marked as the double agent who was getting members of their organization killed, Z Group came up with the plot to eliminate her. They took an oath to keep what they'd done a secret. If KCPD and the Kincaids find out *I* know the truth, then *I'm* the one they'll come after. As far as they know *you* don't even exist!"

"Who's going to find out about us?" The seductive siren had transformed into the devil she was. She reached for his belt and stole another kiss. "Irina's death was the beginning of a whole new opportunity for us to make millions. You weren't worried about Kincaids and repercussions when I first presented the idea of resurrecting Z Group's connections and selling them a new generation of weapons and technology. All you saw were dollar signs. You didn't doubt me then."

He didn't resist when she pushed him onto the bed and climbed on top of him. "I'm not doubting *your* talents. But we flew under the radar for a long time. I'm worried that there are too many people focused on us now."

They continued to undress and take pleasure from each other until he almost forgot the troubles that had brought him to her bed in the first place. Why couldn't it be like this forever? What was the harm in taking the profits they'd already made and buying themselves a small island with no U.S. extradition or tax laws? He rolled her onto her back. "Let's forget the business for a while," he whispered against her ear. "And go someplace warm and sunny. Kansas City is so cold this time of year."

Her hands stilled their exploration and she dropped her head back onto the pillow with an exasperated sigh. "You want to run away?"

He kissed her again, tenderly this time.

She pushed him onto his back and straddled him, reclaiming her power. "I don't run from trouble, dear. I take care of it. Once I learned that John Kincaid was onto our scheme—that he recognized my resemblance to Irina and thought he could build enough proof to destroy me—to destroy *us*—I saw to it that he was taken care of. You didn't have the guts to take down a venerable cop. But I did."

He sat up with her in his lap, as crazy with lust for her as he was annoyed by the jabs to his ego. "You never got John to tell you what he knew or that he'd hidden that information where others could find it, did you? You never broke him."

She adjusted herself in his lap, sheathing her body over his and blurring the lines between argument and passion. "The Kincaids aren't gods. They're just men. I can handle men." She wound her arms around his neck and demanded a kiss. "You just keep giving me what I want. *I'll* keep us safe…" she rocked against him and he knew he was lost "…and make us very, very rich."

Rich. Yes. He pulled her close and let the physical release take him, deciding somewhere between the panting and the sighs that he could lie to the Kincaids a little while longer. Millions of dollars in his pocket could make another headache, a weary conscience, and surrendering control to this woman a risk well worth taking.

HOLLY PUSHED HER SHOPPING BAG, brimming with wrapped presents, to the far end of the booth and slid in beside it. Good. Their food had been served while she'd freshened up in the rest room. "Mmm. That looks and smells delicious."

The warm, rich scents of her prime rib sandwich and au gratin potatoes welcomed her back to the table. So did her sister, Jillian. "Oh, my gosh. These ribs are da bomb." She lifted her fingers to her mouth so that she could speak more politely while she chewed her barbecue pork. "I swear I'm going to gain twenty pounds over Christmas break if you keep feeding me like this. This for sure beats the dorm food I've been eating."

"How often do I get to spoil my little sister?" She'd invited Jillian out for lunch and shopping, partly to make good on her word to Eli about keeping a closer eye on their sister while he was out of the country, but mostly because she treasured rare family moments like this. Ten years Jillian's senior, she'd been forced to play the role of mother rather than sister after their parents had died. She liked playing grown-up friends 100 percent better. "Eat up. I'm going to put you to work back at the apartment while you're staying with me."

"And your idea of work would be…?" Jillian's long brunette ponytail bobbed as she turned her head at an inquisitive angle.

Holly swallowed her bite of the cheesy, creamy

potatoes. "I'm covering so many extra shifts at the lab this week, there's no way I can finish decorating the apartment before Christmas. And you know it's just not Christmas until I get the angel on top of the tree."

"And your ornament village set up."

"And we get Mom's apples and pineapple center-piece put together for the table."

"Fine." Jillian wiped her lips with her napkin and smiled. "I'm up for decorating detail. Just don't ask me to shovel sidewalks or scrape the windshield on any more cars. It's amazing how quickly I've gotten used to going to school in Florida—and how fast all this snow and ice gets old. I enjoyed playing in the snow my first week home, but now…"

Her mock shiver left them both laughing. As they chatted about this and that, plotted what gift to give Eli and finished their meal, Holly soaked in her sister's successful turnaround from her days as an alarmingly skinny teen who'd rebelled in a big way after losing her parents. Once destined for basket-ball scholarships and an all-American life, Jillian had turned to drugs for escape from the pain. The drugs had gobbled up an inheritance and insurance money, gotten her kicked off the basketball team, turned her away from her family and finally landed her in rehab.

Now she was in college working toward a degree in physical therapy. She'd been clean and sober for four years. Jillian was back to a healthy weight, and her self-esteem and mental outlook were equally healthy. Eli didn't have a thing to worry about.

Or did he?

"Here you go, ladies." Their waiter arrived with a tray and set a sauce-covered chocolate cake and a crème brûlée in the center of the table.

"What's this?" Jillian puffed out her cheeks, acting just as full as Holly felt. "Do you want me to work or nap?"

"We didn't order these."

The waiter turned to the side and pointed. "They're compliments of this gentleman. He took care of your meal bill as well. Enjoy."

"Wait a minute." But the waiter was already dashing back into the kitchen to fulfill another order.

Jillian winked. "Do you have a secret admirer?"

"No, I… I think you do."

"Good afternoon, ladies." Holly noted the pricey wool suit before looking up into chiseled features that were a few years older, but just as strikingly handsome as they'd been during Jillian's darkest days. "Mind if I join you?"

Blake Rivers shook his straight blond hair off his forehead and let his Ivy League smile encompass both sisters.

Holly's stunned reaction to the young man's forwardness delayed her response a moment too long. "We were just leav—"

"Sure." Jillian scooted over and patted the seat

beside her. "It's been a long time, Blake. I thought you were off to graduate school at M.I.T."

"I was. Mother and Father insisted I go back and finish my degree." He unbuttoned his jacket and sat next to Jillian, draping his arm along the back of the booth as if they were all old friends.

Holly curled her fingers in her lap, resisting the urge to reach across the table and knock his arm away from its comfortable perch behind Jillian's shoulders. Instead, she bided her time, assessing the clarity of his blue eyes and trying to get a whiff of him beneath the cologne he wore. Her first impression was that he wasn't currently using. But the cologne might be masking the scent of any alcohol he'd been drinking.

Blake's cool blue eyes smiled as though he was aware of her scrutiny—aware that she couldn't find fault with him today. Not like the night when he'd dumped a stoned Jillian off on Holly's apartment stoop and driven back to rejoin a party where they'd both gotten plastered.

Holly tipped her chin and met his silent challenge head on. "So, what brings you back to Kansas City, Blake?"

"I'm working at Caldwell Technologies, in their product development department."

Jillian prompted him to continue. "Sounds interesting."

"I'm in the civilian division, developing a

robotics project. Caldwell Tech also has a military supply division that produces everything from communication and guidance software to experimental weaponry." He dropped his hand down to brush Jillian's shoulder. "If you're interested, we could go out tonight, and I could fill you in on all the details of my work."

The two of them out on the town? No way. "Honey, you can't go clubbing."

Blake answered before Jillian could speak. "You misunderstand me, Holly. I was thinking more along the lines of inviting Jillian to our office Christmas party tonight. Refined company. State-of-the-art catering and decor. The reception is being held at our headquarters building in Lenexa. I think she'd love it. And it would give us a chance to get reacquainted."

Fine. He could play the polite facade, but she needed to remind them of some nitty-gritty facts. "You both have had dependency issues in the past. Don't you think it's a bit risky to attend a party like that? I'm sure there will be alcohol there, and who knows what else?"

Jillian rolled her eyes before sending over a reassuring smile. "C'mon, Holly. That's Eli talking. You can't protect me from every single temptation in the world. I have to live a normal life. And I've been doing that just fine for a long time now. A date with Blake sounds like fun."

"Good. Then it's settled." Blake squeezed

Jillian's shoulders in a sideways hug. "Where are you staying now?"

"At Holly's apartment. Two blocks south of Brush Creek Boulevard."

As Jillian proceeded to recite the exact address and home phone number, Holly realized two things. Her baby sister really had grown up and taken control of her own life. And, she wasn't entirely comfortable with Blake Rivers knowing where she lived. Something about unnamed callers and someone she didn't trust knowing more about her than she did about him left her feeling distinctly unsettled and vulnerable.

But Holly was no longer part of this discussion.

"Do you have a fancy dress?" Blake asked. "Something that will show off those long legs of yours?"

Jillian smiled, more charmed by Blake's confident manner than Holly was. "I think I could dig something out of the closet."

Get her out of this. Say something. Do something. "What about decorating the apartment? You said you'd help."

"C'mon, Holl. We have a week until Christmas, so there's plenty of time to get it done. I promise I won't let you down. Besides, you're working tonight, right?"

"The second half of my split shift, but I can switch—"

"Then you won't miss me if I'm gone." Jillian

turned to Blake and tugged playfully on his lapel. "Do you promise to be on your best behavior?"

"Do you promise to wear some really high heels?"

She laughed. "I'll tower over you, Blake."

"Maybe. But you'll be the hottest woman there, and I'd love to show you off. I can give you a grand tour of the CT building and show you some of the really fascinating stuff we're working on, and we can catch up on old times."

Old times. Exactly what Holly was afraid of. "Jillian," she cautioned one last time.

"Don't worry, Mother Hen." Jillian reached across the table and squeezed Holly's hand. "I can take care of myself now. And I promise to get to the decorating tomorrow."

"Fine. But I'll have my phone on all night. Call me if you need anything." She looked straight at Blake, then back at Jillian. "Anything."

AUTOPSY.

Edward worked his jaw as though he was grinding a toothpick between his teeth. With holiday tunes and the scientific chatter of two lab techs and Holly Masterson filtering through the crisp air around him, he sat at an empty work counter with his arms folded across his chest, staring at the ominous black lettering across the door's reinforced glass.

Although he'd been lying in a hospital bed recovering from a gunshot wound, cuts to his face and torso, broken ribs and a shattered leg when Cara and Melinda had been brought here, he felt the sorrow of the place down to his bones. His father had gone to the morgue that night to identify the bodies and make arrangements for their funeral. Edward had barely been alive enough to attend the double service a few days later, in a wheelchair with a nurse and I.V. at his side.

But he felt them here. His wife and daughter were with him in this room more strongly than he'd felt them in a long time.

Which one of those stainless steel drawers had they lain in? Had André Butler's busted-up body been in the same room with them?

This sterile environment was all facts and logic to the medical examiners and CSIs who worked here, but to Edward, it was a haunting, emotional tomb.

"Earth to Edward."

The subtle scent of something warm and sweet filtered through the memories and pulled him away from the darkness of his past. He wasn't alone. A woman who was very much alive—and very much concerned, judging by the small crease that furrowed her brow—stood beside him.

He pushed his stool away from the counter. "What did you say?"

"Nothing yet. I just called your name. I forget that

this place can really freak visitors out sometimes. Are you okay?" Holly Masterson's voice wasn't come-hither husky, but it was gently articulate, laced with intelligence and practicality—and Edward found its sound a welcome solace to his morbid thoughts. "If it helps, you should know that there's no one in there right now."

Edward spun on his stool and glanced around the lab. He must have been pretty deep inside his head because he hadn't heard the techs leave the room, or sensed the leggy M.E. moving in beside him. He closed the cover of the file he'd been reading. "I was just thinking that my wife and daughter were customers of yours two years ago, almost to the date."

Huh? Where had that come from? He hadn't mentioned that kind of thing to anybody but his therapist and his parents. And now it had popped out in casual conversation with a woman he'd only known professionally until last night. What was wrong with him?

Plenty, Holly seemed to think. She picked up the files he'd been going through and tucked her hand through the crook of his elbow, pulling him to his feet. "If you'd rather sit in my office to read the reports, you can. But I don't want them to leave my lab."

His hand lingered on hers a moment too long when he rose. Though an inexplicable heat radiated between her fingers and his arm, Edward nonetheless pushed her pitying touch aside.

"I can do my job anywhere you…" His gaze

traveled higher than the frown between her eyebrows. Were those…? Resolutely, he forced himself to look into her eyes. "In James McBride's autopsy, you mentioned that an indentation on his right hand indicated he was missing a ring, but…" *Watch the eyes.* "…his attack had been staged to look like a robbery. His family didn't offer any kind of description…" *The eyes.* "Do you know if Detective Grove followed up…?" Nope. He just couldn't look away from the two brown felt antlers sticking up from the top of her head. "Do you mind?"

Without waiting for an answer, he plucked the headband from her hair.

"Hey."

He pushed the Christmas-costume piece into her hand. "I can't have a serious conversation with you when you're wearing these."

"And people tell me *I* can't take a joke," she groused, dropping the headband into the pocket of her lab coat. "It's the holidays. I think we're allowed to indulge in a little goofiness. What *does* make you smile, Detective?"

"I thought we were going with Edward, remember?" Drawn by way of an apology, his hand went back to the staticky ruffs he'd left in her hair. He sifted the short strands between his fingers, combing them back into place. The urge to tangle his fingers deeper into the sable-colored silk took him by surprise, and he quickly pulled away. "There. Much better."

For a long time, he'd thought that Cara's strawberry-blond coloring was the only kind of pretty in the world. But in the past twenty-four hours, he'd been repeatedly distracted by dark brown hair, green-gold eyes and a long, lean figure that had a few surprising curves if a man knew to look for them.

And he'd been looking.

Now he was touching.

Edward lifted his cane from where he'd hooked it over the edge of the counter, giving himself a swift reminder that he was here to investigate his father's murder—to find some new lead that had eluded his brothers and KCPD for too many months. He wasn't here to discover that male blood still pumped through his veins, or that this stick of a woman with the strict rules and Christmas spirit would be the one to jump-start his flatlined libido.

"You didn't answer my question, *Edward*. You do smile, don't you?"

He grinned from ear to ear. "How about that bullet?"

Her laughter softened his mouth into a more honest version of a smile. Nope, he shouldn't be liking that, either. "All right. I can't tell if you're cleverly disarming or ruthlessly persistent. But I'll go get it."

As she went into her office and unlocked a

cabinet, Edward tried to analyze just what was going on here. Months ago, at his father's funeral, he had promised his mother he'd find out the truth. He'd get his dad's badge back into her hands and help KCPD put his killer behind bars. But he wasn't on active duty. He was just supposed to be puttering around behind the scenes, using his free time to dig into things Detective Grove might have overlooked, searching through places his brothers couldn't legally go.

He wasn't supposed to be seizing clues and turning them into leads. He wasn't supposed to be getting closer to the players in the investigation. He wasn't supposed to be feeling that guarded alertness simmering in his veins again, that awareness that an answer could present itself at any moment, and that he needed to have his eyes open wide to see it when it came. That was a cop's way of thinking. Despite what working for KCPD had cost him, he was thinking like a cop again.

That wasn't all that felt foreign to him this afternoon.

When Holly came out of her office and crossed the lab her coltish legs gave a distinctly feminine sway to her hips, and whatever was awakening his long dormant hormones began to steam. She was stubborn and reserved and totally hot. And only a man who was interested in such things should be thinking that way.

He wasn't sure he wanted to be a cop anymore.

He wasn't sure he was ready to be a man who wanted something from a woman.

Yet here he stood, acting like a cop and thinking like a man, unable to look away from the woman who was unintentionally messing with his head.

Holly Masterson, fortunately, attributed his hard stare as interest in the plastic evidence bag she carried.

"Gloves, first." She pointed to the box of disposable gloves like the ones she wore, and while Edward covered his hands, she pulled out a scalpel-like instrument and slit open the labeled bag. She lifted out a sealed glass tube with clear liquid and what looked like a corroded slug from the Civil War inside. "It stays in the bottle. We've got it stored in a vacuum to help retard the decomp process, but it's still extremely fragile."

She laid the bottle in his waiting hands and he lifted it up to the light. With the naked eye, he couldn't see much beyond a gray metal blob. "This isn't from my dad, is it?"

"No. Here, try this." She turned on a halo light and encouraged him to look at the bullet through its magnifying center lens. "These bullets are layered with acid components built in at a microscopic level that react to chemicals inside the human body, speeding the decomp process. This particular bullet is the one that Truman Medical Center took out of your brother Holden two months ago—fired from a gun used by a hired assassin he called Mr. Smith. Unfortunately, the samples I extracted from your father's body are little more than dust now."

As she continued to point out the lack of striation markings and explain the tests they were able to run to verify the caliber of the projectile, Edward clenched his jaw, determined to ignore the way her body brushed up against his and focus on the science she was sharing.

"I'd love to get my hands on a new one that hasn't been corrupted yet—get some baseline data. These disintegrator bullets degrade the surrounding tissues so much that it's hard to get an accurate read on the trajectory and distance of the shot."

"Did you recover any from Mr. Smith's gun?"

She shook her head. "Apparently, this was the last one in his clip when he fired. Your brother and the witness he was protecting covered a lot of territory through a state park when Smith was after them, so it's difficult to narrow down a crime scene and conduct a search. We did recover one bullet from the vehicle they were driving—"

"That would have been the Jeep I loaned him. Man, I miss that car."

"Sorry we had to take it all apart."

Edward straightened on a long exhale and handed her the bottled bullet. "From what I hear, there wasn't much left to take apart."

She resealed the bag with tape and labeled the

time it had been opened with a marker. "That particular bullet had normal degradation after passing through several layers of metal, but it allowed us to pinpoint the caliber. It's up in the ballistics lab right now. We're trying to match it to one of these but haven't come up with anything conclusive yet."

The woman was smart and thorough and… a terrible actress.

Her cell phone rang from one of the deep pockets of her lab coat. Her shoulders stiffened and a soft gasp escaped her lips.

Something was wrong.

She worked on labeling the evidence bag until there was absolutely nothing left to label. Only then did she finally turn her back and reach into her pocket to answer the phone. "Excuse me a minute. Holly Masterson, KCPD crime lab. Hello?"

He should have politely turned away to let her handle the call. Instead, Edward angled himself to watch the color drain from her cheeks.

"Hello?"

Something very cop-like and more territorially male than he'd like to admit sparked along his nerve endings, giving him a clearer picture of the tight press of her lips and the nervous way she reached up to tuck her hair behind her ear.

Her quick smile didn't ring true as she snapped the phone shut and stuffed it back into her pocket. She grabbed the evidence bag off the counter and headed toward her office. "I'd better get this locked back up."

Edward fell into step right behind her. "Is somebody hassling you?"

She shook her head and pulled out her keys. "That call was nothing."

Uh-uh. Not buying it. "Was it the same guy who called you last night at your car?"

Her eyes darted up to his, wide and nearly pure green. But she looked away just as quickly and concentrated on unlocking the evidence cabinet. "There was nobody there. I mean, somebody was there— I could hear him breathing. But he hung up before I could tell him he had the wrong number."

"You didn't want to take that phone call last night, either. You were spooked."

"You were the only thing that spooked me last night." She closed the cabinet, locked it tight then nudged him aside to reach her desk. "It's an annoyance, that's all."

The pale cast to her skin was more convincing than the comment. "How many calls have there been?"

She shuffled through a stack of folders. "You mentioned before that you'd heard about a bullet similar to this one. Your uncle or someone you know makes them?"

"Caldwell Technologies created a prototype disintegrator in their lab. My friend Bill Caldwell says they decided not to manufacture them because there's no viable market. How many calls have you gotten like that one?"

Holly picked up the folders and carried them to a file cabinet. "Caldwell Tech? I know someone who works there." She opened a drawer and thumbed through the tabs. "Is it possible to get a sample of the prototype so that my lab could compare it to the ones from the murder victims?"

Edward reached around her and pushed the drawer shut. "How many calls?"

A heartbeat passed. He inhaled the warm vanilla scent of her hair. A second one passed. If he leaned forward a fraction of an inch, he could nuzzle the long nape of her neck. On the third heartbeat she inhaled deeply and her back pressed into his chest. At the instant of contact, she caught her breath and moved away, half a step closer to the file drawers. "Twenty-seven."

Edward wasn't inclined to move away. "Over how many weeks?" She was frozen, hugging the folder tight to her chest. To heck with it. "Over how many *days*?" When she didn't answer he drew his hand back to cup her shoulder. "Holly?"

Her muscles flinched beneath his touch, but she didn't pull away. "Since I started working the split shifts Saturday night. I've been staying late, re-inputting information from evidence reports that were sabotaged back in April."

He turned her, wanting to read in her eyes that she

didn't think it was an interesting coincidence that the calls had started when she turned her attention to the files Z Group had tried to destroy. "Twenty-seven wrong numbers since you started looking at the Z Group victims again?"

Holly kept her back against the file cabinet. "It's a slow time of year for the lab. It's just what I happen to be working on."

"Are you here alone at night?"

"There are other people in the building."

"But you're alone in the lab?"

"I like the solitude. I get a lot of work done."

"Not when somebody's calling you twenty-seven times." He brushed a strand of mahogany off her cheek, forgetting that he wasn't ready to do the man or cop thing right now. "Did you report the calls?"

"The phone company says someone's probably trying to call whoever had this phone number before me."

"If you told them the number had changed, he wouldn't keep calling. I meant, did you report it to the police?"

Dropping her gaze, she moved one hand from the folders to the middle of his chest where she seemed conveniently fascinated with plucking an invisible thread from the front of his sweater. "Where's the threat in a wrong number?"

"Twenty-seven times in less than a week?" He covered her hand with his own, stilling the manic movements and capturing her chilled fingers against the warmth of his chest. "That's not a wrong number, Stick. That's harassment. Report him."

"'Stick'? Did you just call me 'Stick'?"

"Am I interrupting something?" The spiky-haired lab tech who'd followed Holly into the parking garage last night materialized in her office doorway.

Edward couldn't tell if the kid was embarrassed or concerned. But the speed with which Holly pulled her hand from beneath his reminded him that to an outsider they'd been standing in what probably looked like an intimate embrace. The fact that she slipped so quickly back to her desk reminded him that it had felt like some kind of embrace. The kind of embrace he wasn't ready for.

Scraping his palm over the top of his hair, Edward turned with an irritated huff. "I was just leaving."

But the young man blocked the doorway, his scowl turning into a suck-up smile. "Lieutenant Kincaid, isn't it?" He extended his hand in greeting. "Rick Temple. I couldn't place you last night, but now I do. We met on the André Butler case."

"Rick—" Holly whispered.

"Sorry that I thought you were giving Holly some trouble last night. We never see her with any man around here, so I guess we figured she didn't date."

"Rick, we're not—"

"At any rate, Lieutenant, once I figured out where I'd seen you before, I wanted to apologize. I'm the guy who ran the ballistics tests on weapons you seized from one of Butler's crack houses. We were able to tie the guns to several area crimes. And then you killed the bastard and we ended up not needing any of the—"

"Rick, stop talking." Holly's warning confused the young man into silence and made Edward feel like some kind of weak invalid who needed people to tiptoe around the heartbreaks of his past.

"Did I say something wrong?" Rick asked.

"No, kid." Edward shook his hand and pulled him out of his path in the same movement. What was he doing, getting involved with this woman? With any woman? He'd be lucky if he could make it as a cop again. He didn't need to muddy up the job by getting personal with someone who could wind up getting hurt because of him. "Report the calls," he said on his way out. "I have to go find out about a bullet."

Chapter Five

"Hey, Jamal. Thanks for calling."

Edward was glad to have the chance to stretch his muscles and divert his attention to something other than Holly Masterson's warm scent and frightened eyes. He hefted his cane and then picked it up altogether as he lengthened his stride to cross the crime lab's parking garage in a limping gait that was just short of a jog.

It was about time one of his old street connections he'd called got back to him. "Have you had any luck?"

"Finding your ring? Heck, no."

Edward could imagine the black man's occasional huffs for air meant he was chain-smoking another cigarette, not partaking of any physical activity. It had always amazed him how a man who spent almost his entire day sitting on a bench inside a barbershop could know so much about what was going on in the hidden corners and back alleys of

Kansas City. "Then why are you wasting fifty cents on a pay phone?"

Jamal's croaking laugh turned into a cough. Several seconds passed before he spoke again. "You know, Kincaid—when you tell me to chat up my sources because you're looking for a ring, but you can't tell me anything about what it looks like except that it's gold, that's like telling me to find one particular piece of paper at the city dump. Do you have any idea how many rings are hocked around this city every day?"

"What if I tell you that there may be more than one ring like it? And that it might be designed with or engraved with a Cyrillic Z."

"A what?"

It was Edward's turn to chuckle. "It's fancy foreign writing. Looks like a number three."

"Why didn't you just say a number three?"

"Why don't you just tell me why you called if you haven't heard about any ring."

"I've been hearing some words about your brothers."

"Words?" Edward stopped beside his SUV. After walking so fast, his pulse rate had increased only a fraction, and he wasn't breathing hard at all. The weight training and sobriety were paying off. But Jamal's cryptic comment made his heart beat faster than the physical exertion had. "What do you mean?"

"Well, there's not a brother on the street who doesn't know your daddy got gunned down earlier this year. Folks around here were talkin' about the deputy commissioner's murder for weeks."

A steadying breath kept Edward from flashing back to the pain of his father's funeral. "And…?"

"News about that died down after a while. You know, as one thing or another gets to be more important around here. One of the gangs acts up…or the weather turns or…" Jamal wheezed into another coughing fit. Edward unlocked his Jeep and climbed inside to wait. "You still there, Kincaid?"

"I'm here. Tell me what you heard about my family. If your info's good I'll make a call to guarantee you've got a bed in one of the city shelters every night the weather's bad like this."

"Well, now that's right nice of you. I do hate waitin' in line whenever—"

"Jamal."

"Right. What do I hear about the Kincaids." Edward drummed his fingers atop the steering wheel, mentally bracing for the report. It wasn't unusual for a criminal community that lived and worked on the streets to talk about a certain cop—but usually it was one who walked their beat or was running an investigation on a local crime, or one who was in the news for some reason or another. Talking about an entire family of cops was a different story. "Well, for one thing, somebody's been asking about what your brothers are up to."

"Somebody? Who?"

"Some woman. I haven't had the privilege of talkin' to her myself. I just hear things." A quiet pause indicated he might be lighting up another cigarette. Or that he was about to drop a real bombshell. "It's kinda funny, really. Some woman's out there *asking* what your brothers have been *asking* folks about."

"Hilarious." Whether this woman was keeping tabs on Sawyer, Atticus and Holden's work assignments or looking for something more personal, that kind of scrutiny wasn't a good thing. "Has this woman been asking about me?"

"No. But then you ain't a real cop no more, are you?"

A real cop. His badge and gun were still locked up at home. But if it walked like a cop and talked like a cop… "You haven't mentioned my name to anyone since I called you yesterday, have you?"

"You know me better than that. I'm always discreet."

"Let's keep it that way. I don't want anyone to know that we've been talking."

"If you say so."

Edward turned the key over in the ignition. "Any chance you could get me that woman's name, Jamal?"

"I can do some *asking* myself."

Edward was too busy buckling up and backing out of the parking space to laugh along with him. "Consider your bed reserved."

"I thank you, sir. Anything else I can do for you?"

He punched the Jeep into Drive. "You find me one of those rings, and I'll buy you your own apartment."

HOLLY COULDN'T REMEMBER THE LAST time she'd worn a dress when the temperature was twelve degrees outside. But when she had seen Jillian walk out of the apartment in a red-sequined mini-dress and strappy silver heels, she had had a feeling her Santa Claus sweater and green corduroy slacks wouldn't do the trick. She needed to fit in as a guest at Caldwell Technologies' Christmas party, not stand out as the trespasser she was.

In Caldwell Tech's grand lobby she tugged self-consciously at the hem of her black silk shift and wondered if crashing a party in order to sneak her way into the back rooms of the CT building was the stupidest idea she'd ever had. No, wait—she'd already topped that list this afternoon in her office when she'd nearly burrowed into the inviting warmth of Edward Kincaid's chest.

A swell of compassion at seeing him transfixed by the empty autopsy room had quickly changed into a much more raw emotion when *Unnamed* had decided to call her again. If she'd ever considered the eldest Kincaid son weakened because of his injuries or moods, he'd laid that fallacy to rest. He'd read her fear the way a veteran cop read a suspect who was ready confess. He'd asked her tough questions, given her straight advice and…touched her.

The man had to stand six-three or six-four, had shoulders like Achilles in fighting form, rasped his way through a conversation as though he was some gnarled old character actor—and yet he generated warmth and tenderness the way a gentle, caring man would. He'd earned a reputation as a tough cop who could hold his own with the bad guys in the hidden corners of Kansas City's drug world. And yet the man who'd stroked her cheek and held her hand and calmed her fears had tempted her to forget common sense and decorum, and curl up inside his gentle strength.

"Miss?" Holly snapped herself from her thoughts. Right. Since crashing the Christmas party was mistake number two, it should be a cakewalk by comparison. The man at the refreshment table had asked her a question. "What flavor of hot chocolate would you like?"

Leaving the impulse to tell him to change the "Miss" to "Doctor" on her tongue, Holly smiled. "Amaretto, please."

While the tuxedoed server prepared her nonalcoholic drink, Holly tucked her chin and made a quick survey of the grand lobby, which had been converted into a festive reception area. Built more like a luxury hotel than an office building, Caldwell Tech's marble lobby had been decorated with ever-green trees around its entire perimeter. Each draped with hundreds of white lights, they gave off a piney smell that should have reminded her of the season instead of the fact that her sister Jillian was here somewhere.

Even with the lobby chandeliers dimmed, the place was bright enough to scan the faces of the hundred-plus employees and their guests. Holly wanted to make sure that she spotted Jillian before she or Blake Rivers spotted *her* so that she could avoid an awkward confrontation, an accusation that she didn't trust her sister and was spying on her date—and the whole getting-tossed-out-into-the-snow part when the security guards stationed dis-creetly around the building discovered she was neither employee nor guest.

Some of the women coming through the beveled glass doors of the first floor lobby were wearing fur coats and ankle-length gowns. They paused to greet their host, William Caldwell, a distinguished-looking man with silver at his temples and a serenely beautiful brunette woman by his side. A few of the guests went on to chat with a television reporter Holly recognized from the local news, Hayley Resnick. Though it seemed odd for a woman who seemed to be making a career out of reporting hard news to be at a posh society party, Ms. Resnick certainly fit in with her elegant gown and sparkle of jewelry around her neck.

Holly had managed to sneak in a side door with one of the servers who'd been outside on a break. Now she needed to blend in until she could locate the product development labs and snoop through some computer programs or file cabinets to find out more about bullets that couldn't be traced.

And she needed to do it without running into her sister, a television camera or security—and having to explain herself. Normally, she wouldn't break the rules of etiquette any more than she'd break the rules of the state of Missouri. But when Edward Kincaid had mentioned that William Caldwell's company had made a prototype of the bullet like the ones showing up in so many autopsies, she knew she needed to see one of those bullets, unfired and unscathed.

"Here you go, Miss."

"Thank you." Tucking her evening bag beneath her arm, Holly cradled the cup of hot chocolate between her hands and mimed a few sips to mask her face while she moved through the crowd to the elevator bank. Since she couldn't very well ask for directions to the research section of the building, she'd have to rely on finding a directory and pray that the doors leading to other floors wouldn't be locked.

An hour or so later, Holly was about ready to give up and go home. She'd found her way to CT's development section on the twelfth floor and had been able to go in and out of various offices, which had been left open for an open house tour. Upstairs, the building's marble floors had been replaced with fabricated concrete, which looked modern and aptly state of the art for a technologies company. But the hard surfaces reflected every little sound, so Holly had traded cold toes for stealth, carrying her black pumps with her as she moved from office to office in her stockinged feet, carefully staying out of sight of the visitors taking a tour and the security guards who made routine sweeps of each level.

But her daring impulse was turning into a wasted night. Each of the research labs had been locked up tight and required some kind of pass card or keyed-in code to enter. She'd searched through the open offices, but she lacked the know-how to get beyond their computer network's security system. And all she'd picked up from the file cabinets she'd sorted through was a paper cut. She hadn't found a single schematic or memo about the disintegrator prototype.

Puffing out a sigh that lifted her bangs off her forehead, Holly called up the search command on Blake Rivers's computer one last time. Located at the end of the hall farthest from the elevators and closest to the labs, Blake's office had seemed like the ideal place to hide out while she looked for answers. But none of the logical request words had given her any leads—she'd type in *bullet, ammuni-*

tion, weaponry, disintegrator, bang and *killer.* Not found. Not found. Not found. Nothing. With the evening winding down and her frustration ratcheting up, Holly typed in one last search command. *Z.*

"Then you'd better go back to finding answers through normal channels," she admonished herself. "Science is one hundred percent more reliable than spying." At least for her.

While the computer searched, she tucked her feet beneath her and spun the plush office chair, taking in the cushy digs of a successful young man. More impressive to her than snagging a corner office, Blake's neat space had a private access door to the lab itself. But repeated tries at opening it had proven just as successful as every other dead end she'd reached tonight.

Either through daddy's money, the prestige of an M.I.T. degree or actual hard work, Blake must have proved himself a valuable asset to the company. Maybe she'd done him a disservice this afternoon with her knee-jerk reaction to him asking Jillian to tonight's party. If Jillian had turned her life around after her rebellious teenage years, maybe Blake had transformed himself as well.

Her speculation into Blake's grown-up character ended when a gray file folder icon appeared in the middle of the computer screen. "What the...?" Holly touched her toes to the carpet and stopped spinning. Beneath a row of red *X*'s was a pair of words that sped her pulse and made her think she was finally onto something. *Access Denied*.

Should she print out the screen? What exactly did locating the file prove if she couldn't open it? Should she try to punch in a password? What if a mistake triggered some kind of security alarm or system lockdown?

"Cool it, Holly. Think." She pressed her fingers to her lips and took in a deep breath. Finding a file marked "Z" might not mean anything. "Okay. *Z* doesn't necessarily mean *Z Group*. This is a networked computer system, so the file could be on the server from someone else's work station, not necessarily Blake's. Yet I know he works in development. He'd have access to prototypes."

Trusting the idea that she needed to consult with someone who knew more about this than she did, Holly hit the Print command. She could show the paper to Edward Kincaid—to *Lieutenant* Kincaid. Heck, not only was he a detective, but he was a high-ranking one. Wouldn't running an "unofficial" investigation jeopardize his career? What would happen when he was ready to go back to being a cop? Or didn't he want to be one anymore? He seemed like such a natural. As surprisingly skilled a cop as he was an enigma of grumpy moods and tenderness.

The distinctive beep of the elevator echoed around the corners of the stone hallways. "Someone's showing up now?" The printer whirred as it prepped to produce the single page document. But now that she finally had something to show for her efforts, she could hear the elevator doors opening to the sounds of footsteps and laughter. "You have got to be kidding me."

Giving one last longing look at the private access door to the lab, Holly sprang from the chair and shut off the lights. With only the illumination from the computer screen and the hallway to guide her, she shut down the computer, slipped into her shoes and grabbed her purse, all the while urging the printer to print faster. "Come on."

She at least had to look like a guest checking out the architecture and decor of the place instead of Dr. Snoopy Pants, creeping around where she shouldn't be. "Thank you!"

When the picture of the Z file finally kicked out, Holly stuffed the paper into her purse and ran out the door. If she could reach the supervisor's office two rooms down, where there were professionally designed decorations actually lit up to admire, then she'd have a logical excuse for being up here.

She tried to run on the balls of her feet, but her heels clacked against the floor and made so much noise and, oh, my God—

Laughter. "Blake, stop it." Jillian.

"You stop looking so hot and I'll stop nibbling on your ear. I've got a sofa in my office."

"You said you were going to show me the view of Kansas City from up here."

"You're the only view I want to see."

They were coming this way, straight to Blake's office. Holly mouthed a curse and whirled around, looking for a place to hide.

Automatically, she retreated from the voices and laughter nearing the corner up ahead. She'd better start rehearsing some good excuse or just accept that her sister was going to be pissed off at her for—

A large hand clamped over Holly's mouth as she was lifted from behind and dragged back into Blake's darkened office.

Barely able to breathe, her screams ringing inside her head, she twisted and kicked as the door closed in front of her and the darkness swallowed her up.

Finally, her heel connected with an instep and her captor stumbled. Something long and hard bounced off her knee and onto the carpet.

"Woman, stop fighting me."

The muffled words against her ear were raspy and deep and blessedly familiar. But relief was short-lived. Edward Kincaid must have realized what her suddenly submissive squeaks and squiggles were trying to tell him. Their unwanted company was coming *here*.

"Son of a bitch."

Without releasing her, he carried her to a closet and stuffed her inside. By the time she'd fumbled her way through lab coats and the dark to find the knob, the door was jerked from her hand. She glimpsed a slice of light as the outer door opened a split second before she was pushed against the back wall. The closet door closed and the hand came up to silence her warning cry.

Holly was trapped, pressed from chest to toe between the unforgiving wall and the unmoving body of Edward Kincaid.

"I can feel your heart racing, Stick. It's Ed." He leaned forward and breathed the warning against her ear. "Don't scream. Don't say a word. I'm going to uncover your mouth, okay?"

She nodded, wanting him to understand that she knew who he was, that she'd been unnecessarily startled, but she wasn't afraid.

Well, that last part might not be true, exactly. Her beaded sweater had caught in the nubby tweed of his sweater, pulling it off her shoulder and leaving nothing but a few layers of silk between her body and his. Her heart wasn't the only one racing. Why was Edward here? Why did *he* have to hide?

But questions would have to wait. Blake and her sister had come through the outer office door.

Her initial thought was to simply hold tight to the clutch of wool at his bicep and silently catch her breath and calm her nerves. But he was standing so close, shielding her from prying eyes should their visitors decide they needed something from the closet. Every time she breathed in, she inhaled Edward's clean, leathery scent. Every time his chest expanded, it thrust directly against silk and breasts, hardening her nipples into pebbled nubs. The aroused tips seemed to catch in the weave of his sweater, shooting prickles of desire deeper into her body.

And there was so much heat inside this tiny closet—most of it generated from the man who held her. Scared to death, in the middle of winter—and Holly was on fire from head to toe.

But there was nothing she could do but simmer and breathe and listen.

And she didn't like what she was hearing.

The laughter and conversation out in the office was punctuated with ever-lengthening pauses, hinting that Blake and her sister were making out. A breathy moan and some urgent words confirmed it.

Holly squirmed against Edward's hold, but he wasn't budging. A different, more wary, sort of tension replaced the tautness in her body.

"Okay, Blake, that's enough. Where's this amazing view of the city? You said you could see the glow of the Plaza lights from up here."

"It's a party, darlin'." She heard a soft moist sound that must have been another kiss. "Let's party, already."

"No-o-o," Jillian hummed in weak protest.

So help me, if that bastard thinks he's entitled to something from Jillian…

"Shhh." A voiceless note of calm brushed against Holly's ear.

She squeezed her eyes shut and tried to breathe deeply. But all she got was a noseful of Edward's musky masculine scent and another dose of frustration.

"All right, then, beautiful." Blake was talking again, though he sounded farther away. "We can do it by the window. You enjoy the lights and I'll enjoy you."

Holly dug her fingers into the swell of Edward's arm and buried her face against his shoulder. She didn't want to hear this. She didn't want to be a witness to her sister falling prey to Blake's smooth line and handsome face again. She had to do something.

"I'm not playing hard to get, Blake. I'm saying no." Clutching tighter, Holly silently cheered her sister's firm voice. "We haven't seen each other for four years, and this is all you want? I'm going back to the party. If I see you there, I'll know we're cool. If not…then I'm glad I got to touch base with you. But I don't think you need to call me again."

"Jillian…"

Holly raised her head and listened as the office door clicked open and closed. *Good. Leave that user alone.*

But Blake Rivers wanted what he wanted, and Holly's triumphant smile disappeared. "You've grown up too much like your big sister—an old lady trapped inside a cold fish carcass," he yelled at the closed door. "You used to be more fun than this!" But then a thought must have soothed his temper. "I just have to remind you how good it was between us. I'll put in my time. I like a woman who's a challenge."

Holly didn't hear the insult as much as she heard the determination in Blake's voice.

"That's my sister. I have to warn—" But suddenly Edward's lips were pressed against hers, short-circuiting both her thoughts and her voice. At first, they functioned like the same hard, unmoving muzzle his hand had been, but then...

The outer door opened. "Wait up, Jillian," Blake called. "I'll walk you back downstairs."

The threat of discovery left the room, the outer door closed and Holly breathed a guarded sigh of relief. With a crowd of guests serving as a visible audience, Blake Rivers wouldn't be able to pursue the "challenge" of bedding her sister.

With the sigh, her lips parted and squeezed together, brushing against Edward's mouth in an unintended mimic of a kiss. Suddenly, every sense was focused on the point where their lips met. That innocent caress felt like the sweetest, most dangerous thing she'd ever done. As tender as a first kiss— as risky as waking a sleeping dragon.

Edward's mouth moved against hers and Holly held her breath. He was tentative at first, almost as if he was testing to see if their lips were really touching. "Holly?"

Was he looking for her to either welcome him or push him away? Dragon or prince? She'd always had a penchant for the more magical of the two.

In a heartbeat, the needy woman inside her made her choice. She licked her lips and whispered his name. "Edward."

With no other magic than that, she'd loosed the dragon. Edward's mouth opened silently, hotly, firmly over hers. With a hand bracing the wall on either side of her head, his chest and thighs still pinning hers, he thrust his tongue between her lips and forced her to open wider beneath his sensual assault. He slid his tongue along hers, and she tasted her own chocolate drink on him. He gently suckled the swell of her bottom lip between his teeth, drawing pinpoints of fire to that sensitive spot. When she moaned in pleasure at the heady spell he was casting over her, he plunged in again, kissing her with a raw need that was as powerful as it was exhilarating.

Trapped as she was, Holly could only curl her fingers into the front of his sweater and hold on as he plundered her mouth and she tried to return the favor. By the time he'd tunneled his fingers into her hair to pull her away from the wall and tip her head back to brand her cheeks and eyes and lips with more hungry kisses, Holly was breathing hard, boiling over and unaware of anything except the needs of this man and the needs spreading like a flash fire through her own body.

"No way…" Edward grimaced against her mouth, kissed her again. He raised his head, sucked in a deep breath, then leaned in to gently rub his grizzled cheek against her softer one. "…are you a cold fish. You're…you're…" He squeezed her shoulders and set her firmly back against the wall. It was too dark to read the expression in his eyes, but his ragged breathing washed over her in warm, uneven waves. "I didn't want to kiss you."

Not what she'd expected him to say. Holly desperately tried to focus. What was going on here? What just happened? How could a man just turn his passion off like a switch? She was still reeling with it. "You didn't want…?"

"Holly…"

She shoved him aside and fumbled with the doorknob, embarrassed that her lips felt bruised and swollen, embarrassed that she couldn't catch a deep breath—embarrassed that she wanted him to kiss her again. "Well, Merry Christmas to you, too."

"Don't say that." His steadier hand reached around her and twisted the knob open.

Holly pushed open the door and stumbled out into the room on legs that trembled like gelatin. "Don't say 'Merry Christmas'? Who are you, Ebenezer Scrooge with a badge and an attitude?"

While Holly tugged her sweater back into place, Edward limped up beside her on his cane. Masquerading as some wounded veteran of life. Ha! He'd just proved very convincingly that his big, bad body was working on all cylinders. It was just his personality that needed the crutch. "Those words have meaning to me. I can't stand to say them or hear them tossed out in anger like that."

"Don't get righteous with me, Lieutenant. They mean something to me, too. I was just dishing out the same sarcasm as you were throwing." But maybe she was prodding the dragon too far. The grim line of his mouth was set too tight, and his deep gray eyes burned from the shadows. She ignored the tug at her heart, gathered her pride and opened the door. "Fine. We'll leave it at you didn't want to kiss me. Stupid mistake on my part, too."

"Holly." See? The man with the cane could really move when he wanted. He caught up to her in the hallway and touched her arm. She shrugged him away and marched toward the elevators. "Holly, it was an accident."

"How can you accidentally kiss somebody?"

"It wasn't the right time to do it." So there would be a right time? A frisson of anticipation fizzled out when he grabbed her hand and pulled her to a stop.

When she couldn't slip away a second time, she pulled up straight on her high heels and looked him in the eye. "Making out in the closet wouldn't have been my first choice for a romantic interlude, either. But it takes two willing participants to make something like that happen."

His steel gray eyes darkened and narrowed. "I meant I don't want you to go playing spy-girl again. You nearly got caught."

"*You* were playing spy-boy."

"*I* know what I'm doing."

She twisted against the grip on her elbow. "Apparently, you didn't know it when you were kissing me."

"Who'd have thought a sweet thing like you would have such a smart mouth." He released her and Holly spun around and headed toward the elevators. But the tap of his cane followed closely behind her. "Trust me. I knew exactly what I was doing when I kissed you. That bastard's insult was way off base about you—I want you to know that. I didn't want you to cry out to tell him where to get off. And then I got carried away when I should have been thinking about your safety. I guess I'm more out of practice with this man-woman thing than I realized." He was right beside her when Holly reached the elevators and pushed the call button. "I've been here before as a guest of my dad's friend, Bill Caldwell. I know how to get around this place and what I'm looking for. I know how to *not* get caught."

"I wouldn't have gotten caught," she insisted.

"Your sister and her boyfriend almost spotted you in the hall, and then you darn near revealed yourself to get them to stop making out. She sounded like she was a grown woman, like she could handle herself. She didn't need your interference."

"I wouldn't be talking about interference if I were you, pal." Holly hugged her purse tightly to her chest, staring resolutely at the steel elevator door. But then she considered that an explanation might serve better than a snappy comeback. "I have reason to be concerned about Jillian. There are issues you don't know about. In high school, after our parents were killed in a plane crash, she got herself into trouble. Got hooked on cocaine. Party-boy Blake back there was one of her main co-dependents. He had the money for whatever she wanted as long as she gave him a tumble." She tucked a stray lock of hair behind her ear and held it there, fighting back the painful memories of sleepless nights and constant worry. "You don't know what it's like living with someone who has an addiction. You want to watch over them all the time. You want to protect them from themselves and from anyone who wants to take advantage of that weakness."

Holly waited in uncomfortable silence for his response to the revelation of how her dysfunctional family dynamic worked.

The elevator arrived, the doors opened and Holly stepped inside. Edward pushed the lobby button and retreated to the opposite corner before he finally spoke.

"Trust me, Stick. I can tell you anything about addictions you want to know." She slid him a sideways glance. His eyes were focused on a distant place. "You can love your sister to death and try to protect her all you want, but in the end, she has to fight her battles herself or she'll never control the monster."

"The monster?" Jillian had used that term before.

Edward's gaze rose to meet hers, shrinking that distance between them. "I have a feeling, after a screwed-up night like this one, I'll need to go to an AA meeting."

Holly relaxed her defensive stance. "You're an alcoholic?"

"Recovering. I've been clean and sober for eight months." His chest expanded and fell with a gut-deep sigh. "Explains a lot about me, huh?"

She took a step toward his corner of the elevator. "I didn't know. Eight months." Holly clicked off the numbers in her head. "That's since your father's murder. That's a wonderful tribute to him. Congratulations."

For a moment, he seemed taken aback by her compassion. But then his mouth set in a grim line, and he thumped his cane in his hand. "I can't lose anyone else. I can't start to care and lose anyone again. Is that clear?"

Did that mean he cared about her? Holly took another step. "So, now who's being overprotective and not letting someone fight her own battles?"

"This is different. Z Group is different." He

thumped his cane in his palm a second time. "You leave bending the rules and risking somebody's neck up to me. You stay in your lab where it's safe, and everything will work out just fine."

"You're sacrificing your career—maybe even your life—for this case? I thought you didn't want to lose anything else."

"Don't get smart with me and twist my words around."

"Then say what you mean." Now that she wanted eye contact, he wouldn't look at her. She touched his chin and turned his face to her. "Let me see— you don't like to say 'Merry Christmas…'" He pulled his chin away, but she cupped his strong jaw and kept him facing her. "You don't like kissing women in closets, you don't like anyone hinting that you're a good cop whom KCPD could still use and you don't like admitting when you have feelings for someone." Holly stroked her thumb across his lips, thinking about reawakening his dragon's heart with another kiss. The elevator hit a gentle bump and slowed its descent. "Am I pretty clear as to what your words are telling me?"

Edward turned his whole body toward her, huffing up. He opened his mouth, about to deny the truth.

But the elevator doors slid open and a woman's voice spoke from the lobby. "Edward?"

The party's host, and Caldwell Technologies'

owner, William Caldwell, braced the doors open with his hand. He looked every inch the wealthy entrepreneur and power broker she'd read about in the papers—from his hand-tailored tuxedo to the polished gold pinkie ring he wore. But it was the elegant brunette on his arm who'd spoken.

Holly quickly snatched her hand from Edward's face. This was what "caught" felt like. Now she was about to be escorted off the premises—if not hauled away in a police car.

Perhaps sensing her urge to bolt, Edward's hand clamped down over her wrist. He pulled her off the elevator beside him. "Mom."

Mom? Holly felt her eyes bug open. This was his mother?

The dark-haired older woman stretched up on tiptoe and exchanged a hug and a kiss with Edward. "I didn't know you'd changed your mind about coming tonight, sweetie. Does this mean you'll be at the house for Christmas Eve, too?" Holly had managed to wipe the shock off her face by the time the woman turned to greet her with a warm smile. "Hi. I'm Susan Kincaid, Edward's mother. Are you a friend?"

She could see the resemblance now—the bone structure around the cheeks and eyes, the dark brown hair—though hers was peppered with streaks of gray. Taking Susan Kincaid's hand, she completed the introduction. "Holly Masterson. I'm…"

What was she? Accomplice in crime? Confessor? Closet make-out artist?

"She's an M.E. from the crime lab, Mom." Edward's gruff voice answered the question for her.

"Oh." The small lines beside Susan's dark eyes creased with disappointment. But just as quickly, her expression perked up again. She beamed a smile at her son. "You're working?"

Mr. Caldwell lifted his chin, looking curious to hear the answer to that one, too. "Have you finally decided to go back to KCPD, son? Or are you moonlighting on your father's murder investigation?"

Edward's grip on her wrist tightened and he muttered under his breath. "I definitely need to find a meeting."

Chapter Six

Edward pulled his stocking cap low over his ears and turned up the collar of his coat to keep the newly-falling snow from drifting down the back of his neck.

"You're going to do the right thing, aren't you, Daddy?"

There were bad nights when Edward couldn't fathom why he'd been left alive when the two people he'd loved the most had been taken from this world. And then there were ones that were off-the-chart crazy like this one, and he had a sneaking suspicion that learning to cope with beautiful, headstrong, insightful, vulnerable, well-meaning, complex, troublesome, stubborn women like his mother and Holly Masterson was actually some kind of cosmic punishment for failing his family.

"Yeah, baby, I'm gonna try," he muttered into the freezing air. "I'm going to try."

"What's that?" Though covered by a long dress coat, Holly's delectable bottom bounced like forbidden temptation as she backed out of the rear seat of her Honda. Edward sternly tipped his face to the black sky and the snow that seemed to be falling straight from the lights towering over Caldwell Technologies' parking lot. She straightened with the scraper-brush she'd gone fishing for in her hand and matched his stance, squinting up into the falling snow. "Is it getting worse?"

Edward wished he could have explained to his daughter what it cost a man to be a gentleman sometimes. But Melinda never would have understood. Her world had always been black and white. Good and evil. Daddy was a good guy, so he would separate work to be done from the pleasure to be had in kissing Holly again.

He'd let his mother think that his life was getting normal enough to attend a party with a female friend again. But the truth didn't sound much better. Um, no Mom, I'm not dating—I'm following up a lead on a case I'm not really supposed to be working on because, you know, I'm not really a cop anymore and, oh yeah, the potentially incriminating evidence I found here tonight might just point to our old family friend who seems to be becoming much more than a friend to you since Dad died.

Explain those kinds of complications to an eight-year-old girl with Down's syndrome.

He wasn't sure he could explain them to himself. So he plucked the scraper from Holly's hand and said, "Looks like it." As she closed the back door, he opened the front one for her. "You sit inside while the engine's warming up and I'll brush the snow off your windows."

"You've walked me to my car to make your mom happy, kept me from blowing my cover with Mr. Caldwell and snuck me out of the building without my sister or Blake Rivers seeing me. I think I can scrape my own car." She closed the front door, sending an avalanche of snow down over the tops of her high heels. Her face froze for a moment in mute shock. Almost instantly, the icy crystals started to melt and seep inside her shoes. Her toes would be frozen in a minute if they weren't already. "Really, I can."

Edward was too tired to wipe the amused smirk off his face at her deadpan delivery. "Allow me." Shifting his balance, he went down on his good knee in front of her and brushed the snow off her feet. He was still smiling when he stood back up. "Now, will you get in the car and let me work?"

"Why do you carry a cane?" she asked in lieu of "I'd love to get warm, thanks." "You don't need to use it. You knelt down just now without any problem. When you dropped it in Blake's office, you still managed to toss me into the closet and then run back and get it without missing a beat. From everything I've observed, your body has healed."

She couldn't just get in her car, could she.

Edward gave up on smiling and went with the logical explanation. "It's for that one time my knee or ankle gives out or I hit a patch of ice and I slip. I'm not going back to the hospital because vanity kept me from using a cane to balance myself."

One dark brow arched beneath her snow-dotted bangs. "Sounds like an excuse to me."

"Yeah, well, the cold air makes my joints ache like a big bear, so I'm using the cane."

Holly shrugged. "I'm not an orthopedic doctor, but your limp is barely discernible, your reflexes are quick and you have enough musculature on your body to compensate for any minor shifts in balance. Have you tried to pass your active-duty physical since you were injured?"

He tried glaring her into the car.

A knowing smile bloomed across her face. "You passed the physical already."

If she asked about the mental exam, this conversation would be over. It needed to be over. "It's something my physical therapist has me go through every month so she can benchmark my progress."

Holly plunged her gloved hands into the pockets of her coat. She was shivering. "Jillian is studying to be a physical therapist."

This was ridiculous. "If I hand over my cane, will you get in the car before you freeze?"

As usual, she had one more thing she wanted to say. She clutched her collar together at her neck and lightly stamped her feet. "I knew the party was going on tonight because of my sister. I wanted to get in here and see one of those bullets you mentioned. But I also wanted to check on her. I mean, I didn't want her to know I was checking on her, but I was worried because of her history with Blake."

Her tongue darted out to nervously moisten her lips. Edward's gaze darted to the spot and something needy growled inside him. *He* was having no problem staying warm.

"I just wanted to thank you for listening to me— for reminding me that I can't be such an overprotective sister that I start enabling her addictive behavior again." The fingers at her collar reached out and brushed against his chest, lightly petting him while she sought her next words. When she curled her fingers beneath the placket of his coat, he wished there weren't gloves and coats and sweaters between them. "Thank you for telling me about your addiction, too. Sometimes I forget that other people can understand what my family has gone through. It's good to be reminded I'm not alone."

That better be snow melting on the tips of her lashes. Even before she blinked away the sheen of tears, the urge to kiss a smile or defiant pout or any other expression but sadness onto her lips surged through him. Edward dipped his head and pressed his mouth to hers, taking a gentle kiss. He angled his head the opposite way and kissed her again, kissed her until he'd warmed away the chill from her lips and she was kissing him in return.

But when the need to feel her long curves aligned against his harder angles had him backing her into the car to deepen the kiss into something that was more passionate than healing, Edward reluctantly pulled away. He stepped back far enough to let the wintry air surge between them and cool his randier impulses. His breath might be stuttering inside his chest and his jeans might be feeling a little tight behind his zipper, but he was going to be a gentleman. He was going to be a good guy.

"So…" he began gruffly. Holly's cheeks were flushed with more than the cold and he had to look away or his good intentions might go to hell. Plucking the scraper from her unresisting grasp, he went to work cleaning the snow off her windshield. "…you infiltrated Bill Caldwell's party because you wanted to see if you could get some information on one of those bullets."

She cleared her throat. "Yes. But I couldn't get into any of the labs. I knew Blake Rivers worked in product development, so I thought if I could get into his office I might be able to find a schematic or chemical recipe for the bullet to see how they decompose so quickly. Wait." With a little more energy to her voice, she opened the car door and pulled a crumpled sheet of paper from her purse. "I did find this on Blake's computer. Actually, it was on the network server, so it could belong to anyone in the company, but..." She smoothed out the paper against her thigh and handed it to him. "There's a coded file marked 'Z'. Now it could mean projects made with zinc or an employee named Zach, but I thought the coincidence was too much to ignore since we've traced similar bullets back to Z Group."

"May I keep this?"

Holly nodded. "I wish I could have gotten my hands on one of those bullets. There are so many things the lab could find out if I could compare just one that wasn't tainted to the decomposed bullets."

Edward pulled off a glove and lifted his coat to fold the print-out into the pocket of his jeans. Then he dug deeper and pulled out a small plastic bag. "You mean one of these?"

Holly's face lit up like Christmas d—no, he didn't even want to think that comparison. "Is that a disintegrator? How did you get your hands on one?"

"It helps to be friends with the boss. One of the guards recognized me as a friend of Bill's, and I talked him into letting me tour a lab."

She ducked and weaved like a prizefighter, trying to look at the inch-long projectile from all angles without touching the bag. "I don't have any examination gloves with me. The fibers from these wool ones would transfer too easily."

"Lord, woman, you'd think I'd brought you chocolates or flowers."

Her green-gold eyes glanced up at his. "Trust me, this is better. May I see it?" Without pressing her fingers against the bullet inside, she lightly took hold of one corner of the plastic bag and examined the contents more closely. "So, you stole this, huh?"

"There were boxes of them in Rivers's storage locker."

"Boxes?" She frowned without looking away from the specimen she held. "I thought you said Caldwell Technologies had created a prototype."

Seeing hundreds of them inside that storage locker had bothered him, too. "That's all it was supposed to be. I don't know if these are new or have been sitting there for a while, but the bullets have definitely been put into production at some time. I'll wait for a more private moment to ask Bill about them."

"Or Blake Rivers. You said they were in his storage locker?"

Edward nodded. "Rivers could be manufacturing them on the side and selling them under Bill's nose. I'll see what I can find out. Do you have a way to compare this bullet to what's left of the ones at your lab?"

"Yes."

"Maybe someone here is supplying the ammunition Z Group is using to kill its former operatives in Kansas City." Edward glanced around the parking lot to make sure no one was eavesdropping on their conversation. But since they'd departed the festivities early, they appeared to be alone. "According to my dad's journals, the organization is responsible for some major arms smuggling. If these do match up to the slugs taken out of the victims, then there may be other types of weapons and technology being produced at Caldwell and shipped out of the country."

"But this it isn't a legal seizure of evidence." Edward stifled a groan. Couldn't Holly see that following the rules and obeying strict investigative protocols hadn't solved any of the murders yet? "If we do prove a connection, we couldn't use it in court," she continued.

"One step at a time, Stick." He opened her car door, tossed the scraper onto the floor behind the front seat, then stepped aside for her to climb in behind the wheel. "Let's make a connection first, and then we'll get nitpicky with the details. What if I'd told you that I found that in Rivers's trash can?"

"Did you?"

He kept a straight face through the lie that would temporarily absolve them of guilt. "Yes. Now quit smiling at me like that. Call me tomorrow, and let me know what you find out on that bullet."

"I will." She reached across the space between

them and squeezed his hand. "Good luck finding your meeting. Take care of yourself."

He squeezed back. "You, too."

Edward closed the door behind her, brushing some snow off the side window as she shifted the car into Reverse. Then he patted the roof of the car, letting Holly know she was clear to back out of the parking space.

He watched the silver Honda until it turned onto the access road. Then he hunched his shoulders against the cold and headed toward his Jeep, carrying his cane in his hand.

"Good job, Daddy. Good job."

Was that his conscience congratulating him for letting Holly drive away without forcing more of his conflicted feelings and desires on her?

Or was his little girl's voice—and some rusty investigating instincts—telling him he was finally on the right track toward solving his father's murder?

HOLLY WASN'T SURE IF IT WAS fear that she'd be caught or just flat-out excitement that she'd finally gotten her hands on an intact disintegrator bullet that made her drive away from the Plaza lights and her apartment and toward the crime lab facility.

She'd always done her best thinking alone in her lab at night when there were fewer interruptions from coworkers and fewer calls to crime scenes. The quietness of the building and the sleeping world beyond its walls seemed to soothe her nerves and free up her powers of observation and concentration.

Tonight was no different. She'd dumped her coat in her office and kicked off her high heels. She wore the black silk dress with a hand-beaded sweater underneath her lab coat. But the rest of the trappings that put her in a productive mental groove were the same.

With Julie Andrews singing Christmas carols through her headphones, her plastic goggles and gloves on, and her metal clipboard on the countertop beside her so she could jot notes, Holly quickly lost herself in her work. Though she wasn't the ballistics expert Rick Temple was, she knew the basics about testing for chemical components and running reaction tests. Using sample scrapings from the unfired bullet, she'd already determined a few fundamental facts—the metal jacket was partly fabricated with a dense ceramic compound. And while that compound was resistant to physical stress, it had a tendency to break down quickly when combined with certain chemicals.

A saline solution similar to human tears had no effect. The chemicals in sweat, nothing.

But something inside the human body turned that rock-hard object into mush in a matter of hours. And there were plenty of chemical combinations left to try.

Holly had lost track of the hour by the time she walked out of the lab's sample bank for blood and tissue. "Glo-o-o-o-o-or-ia…"

She stopped by Rick Temple's office and wrote out a note requesting a favor. Could he provide a list of chemical compounds that would be resistant to the minute gunpowder explosion that fired a bullet from a gun? Since he was so keen on proving who between the two of them was smarter, she'd give him the chance to strut his stuff.

Maybe he could narrow down whether it was a man-made agent or a naturally occurring element that kept the bullet from blowing up inside the gun when fired, yet made it soften like putty when exposed to something inside the human body. Then she dropped the note and a copy of the sample bullet's chemical component graph into an envelope and tucked it inside his desk. No sense leaving it in his work-order job box since this would have to be an off-duty request.

Mindlessly singing along with the CD, Holly waved at Floyd at the front desk and hurried back down the stairs so she could prep her next reaction experiment. Holding a vial of a minute fragment of the bullet suspended in solution, she injected a sample of O positive blood, mixed them together in a centrifuge and waited for something to happen.

She counted off the reaction in seconds. Before a minute had passed on the clock above the door, the solution had clouded over. Within another minute, it was clearing again.

"And we have lift-off!"

A tremor of excitement fed her energy and she picked up her clipboard to record the time and her observations. She'd need to get one of the actual chemists to run a comparison analysis on this solution and the remains of the decomposed bullets she'd extracted from one of the Z Group victims to see if they were an exact match or just a similar product. And then they'd need to break down the components in the blood to see if it was the iron or—

Holly slammed the clipboard down on the counter. What was she getting so excited about? Nobody was going to run any such test.

She reached into her pocket and turned off her music, her Zen-like focus busted over one simple, but very important fact. "You're an illegal bullet."

Unless she or the detectives working the case could come up with some other plausible reason to obtain a warrant, there was no going back to Blake Rivers's lab and proving the stash of bullets Edward had found was part of Z Group's smuggling business or enforcement operations.

She pulled off her headphones and let them hang around her neck. What she had here was, at most, proof that would satisfy her own curiosity about untraceable bullets, and at least, a vial of red dish water.

Maybe Edward could take this information and do something with it. She was a doctor, not a detective. She could provide the science, but someone with a badge had to put it into context and drum up a suspect to turn her research results into a case.

Now that the adrenaline rush of her search was ebbing, she was seized by a yawn that made her extremely cognizant of the long hours she'd been keeping these past few days. She actually made note of the time, and not the passage of it, when she looked at the clock again. It was going on 2 a.m.

Sensible people would be in bed asleep. What had happened between her and Edward tonight—from passion-laced kisses to covering each other's story for crashing the Caldwell party to the revelation of intensely personal secrets—might not qualify as sensible, but they'd certainly felt…inevitable.

The urge to call him—to connect with him again, even over a phone line—pulsed within her. True, she wanted to tell him about her findings with the bullet that he'd found in the "trash" and share her frustrations over producing a solid lead and a dead end at the same time. But more than that, she craved the sound of his throaty, sexy voice. Whether they were butting heads, sharing secrets or exchanging comforts, there was something as uniquely soothing and stimulating about his voice as there was to the intimate quiet of the night she loved so well. She wanted that voice to tell her if that second kiss in the parking lot had been as "accidental" as the one in the closet had been.

But Edward had been serious about finding an AA meeting, and she certainly couldn't intrude on that. Maybe that's what she needed—an organized support system that could help her sort through emotionally confusing nights like this one. She hadn't found anything so earth-shattering that it couldn't wait until morning. And just because these feelings for Edward Kincaid had hit her hard and fast didn't mean he felt the same way—or even wanted to feel the same way.

"Go home, Holly," she advised herself since she *was* the sum total of her own support group. Despite Edward's advice that she needed to let Jillian fight her own battles, Holly wanted to make sure her sister had made it home safely from the party. Plus, a few hours of sleep wouldn't hurt her, either.

Already gathering her samples and straightening her work station, Holly vowed to wait until a more humane hour to call Edward. She glanced up at the clock and smiled, amused by her own coy thoughts. Maybe she could put her curiosity and hormones on hold until, oh, say, eight in the morning?

The flicker of a shadow floating past the translucent glass drew her attention to the door. She caught her breath on a strangled whisper. "Not again."

As the initial, short-lived terror of being startled

fired through all her senses and then burned itself out, Holly stared at the clouded glass, waiting for the shadow to reappear. Her eyes burned before she finally blinked.

She heard no sound, saw no more movement. Maybe there was a problem with the stupid lights out there. Or maybe… Holly planted a fist on one hip and her clipboard on the other. "Rick? Is that you? These games of yours are way past old. I'm going to write you up if you don't show yourself right now."

But there was no laughter, no teasing voice that answered. Her defiance quickly waned as a dozen other explanations—none of them good—flashed through her mind. As she eased her white-knuckled grip on the stainless clipboard, the aloneness that had seemed so relaxing a short while ago rushed in on her, making her frighteningly aware of her isolation.

Rationalize this, Holly. Solve the mystery. Make it go away.

She tried to reason with her paranoia. Other people worked at the lab through the night. There were at least a six technicians on the late shift, plus cleaning staff. There were guards on duty at each entrance and one who did routine patrols. She should call Floyd at the main desk just to verify that one of his officers was patrolling the basement level right now.

She wasn't alone. She could call for help. She repeated the phrase, "I am not alone." Anyway, the shadow had disappeared. Maybe the movement had even been a figment of her weary imagination. She'd been awake so long that distinguishing fantasy from reality was getting—

A dark shape suddenly filled the door frame and Holly backed into the counter, knocking over a rack of vials. There was no reasoning with her fear. "I'm calling security," she warned, pushing away from the counter and forcing her feet to move toward her office where she could put a locked door between her and the intruder.

Holly never reached her office.

The door swung open. She glimpsed a black sleeve reaching in before the lab was plunged into darkness. The footsteps charging toward her sounded louder than her cries for help. Holly ran toward her office, knocked her shin against a rolling cart, tipping cart and contents onto the floor.

As she stumbled to find her footing again, a bright light flashed in her eyes, blinding her for the seconds it took her assailant to cross the room. A shadow loomed up that was blacker than the darkness surrounding it. Arms reached for her. Holly screamed, hurled her clipboard at the shadow's chest and ran. But her stockinged feet offered little traction on the linoleum floor. The narrow beam of light shifted, shining straight up to the ceiling.

Then the light itself seemed to attack. Fire

exploded in the side of her skull and Holly crumpled to her hands and knees.

She clawed at the arms that tried to pick her up, but could find no purchase, and soon enough the black hands gave up their effort and left her in a pile on the floor. She blinked through the pain swirling round inside her skull. There were dark spots on her lab coat. Huh? Was that blood staining the sleeve? She must have broken the vial she'd been testing and compromised the sample. No. Wait. Hadn't she left the sample on the counter? *Make sense of this, Holly. Make sense.* But the room heaved and she couldn't think. Her eyes wouldn't focus. Her stomach rolled. She couldn't hold her head up.

She flopped over onto her side and the deadly light swept across her arm. Wait a minute. That was *her* blood.

But the moment of clarity passed and her brain shut down.

The last thing she remembered was watching her feet slide along behind her across the floor of the autopsy lab. She was going somewhere, except her legs weren't moving. And then…

Blackness.

HER PHONE WAS RINGING.

Holly's head felt heavy on her pillow. She must have crashed hard by the time she got home and crawled into bed. If she kept her eyes closed and pretended to be in a deep sleep, maybe Jillian would get it.

It rang again.

She slit one eye open in the darkness. Who was calling so early? *Come on, Jillian. Please.*

Another ring. The second eye opened.

Why was it so cold in her apartment? Had Jillian burned the toast again and opened a window to let the smoke out?

She couldn't smell anything burning. What she smelled was something faintly antiseptic. She must have worn her lab coat home again. But why was she sleeping in it?

"Jillian?"

One croaky word and shards of pain pierced her skull.

Holly tried to roll over to read the clock on her bedside table, but her hand hit the bedpost and fell back to her side. She couldn't turn. Nausea welled up in her stomach, and Holly decided lying perfectly still was the only option if she wanted to keep her last meal down. *Jillian, please.*

Ring.

"Darn it." Ignoring the pain and queasiness the movement caused her, Holly reached for the phone.

But her knuckles rapped against steel, not wood. What the...? She splayed her hand flat against the chilled surface. Where was she?

Uncertainty quickened her pulse. Certainty made it race.

Her cell phone was ringing in her pocket. Taunting her with its relentless repetition. Waking her to the nightmare of her surroundings.

"Oh, my God," Holly squeaked, raising her hand. She hit flat steel, only a few inches above her face. "No." Steel to her right. Steel to her left. She reached over her head. More steel. "Help me."

She was lying inside one of the steel autopsy drawers.

Wide awake now, she knew the pain throbbing inside her head would be a minor thing if she couldn't get her panicked breathing under control. She tried to count to three—telling herself to breathe in through her nose and out through her mouth. *Stay calm. There's plenty of air in here.*

But she had to get out. "Help?"

She knocked on the walls. "Help me!" Her cries bounced off the sterile walls and came back to mock her. She tried to brace her feet against the wall and push the drawer open. But there was no traction for her stockinged feet. Holly pounded her fists against the opening, flinching as each sound rang like a cymbal crash through her skull. "Somebody, help me!"

And the phone kept ringing.

"Stop it!"

The panic was winning as she twisted around

and pulled at her lab coat and finally reached her pocket. Her eyes watered as she fought to bring the blurry lighted screen of her cell phone into focus.

Unnamed.

Holly answered the phone. "Why are you doing this? Why?"

For a few seconds, the relaxed breathing at the other end of the call was the loudest sound inside her metal coffin.

And then she started screaming.

Chapter Seven

Edward reached the second-floor banister railing of Holly's apartment building, feeling the unfamiliar nerves of boyish energy. But he wasn't sure if it was silly pride over climbing the two flights of stairs without the use of his cane, or trepidation that he'd actually followed the impulse to drive over to Holly's apartment this morning.

But he was thirty-five, a widower, and long past feeling boyish. So he took a deep breath and set off in search of apartment 212.

He had a perfectly rational reason for being here that had nothing to do with persistent thoughts about long legs and silky hair and kisses that were waking something more profound than lust in his system. Holly said she'd call him today with results from her tests on the disintegrator bullet, and since she hadn't answered at her office or her cell phone, she must still be at home. Okay, so it was a little early to be making a house call, but if he promised coffee and breakfast, maybe he could get her to the lab and get his results sooner.

And the idea of a few sparks flaring up over the course of their breakfast conversation had gotten Edward out of bed with a purpose this morning. The chance for another face-to-face meeting with Holly Masterson had gotten him shaved and dressed and looking forward to this bright, snow-packed day more than he had any other day for a long time.

At last night's AA meeting, they'd talked about living in the moment. He'd learned to do that as the father of a special needs child. Now he was learning how to do that all over again. With his painful past and uncertain future temporarily blocked from his mind, he was determined to live in *this* moment. And at this moment, he wanted to see Holly.

208. 210. 212.

He hesitated in front of the aged walnut door, trimmed in evergreen garland and candy canes. The Christmas cheer just didn't quit with this woman, did it. *"Don't wimp out, Daddy. Do it!"*

"Okay, baby. I'm doing it." Ignoring the trappings, he focused on the center of the solid wood and knocked.

He immediately heard shuffling noises from the other side, and a voice that was not quite familiar. "Okay, well, sorry to load up your voice mail, but call when you get this. Please." Then, "Yes?"

Now the voice was talking to him. "Holly?"

"Who is it?" Not Holly. The peephole in the door darkened as an eye looked through it.

"Are you her sister, Jillian?"

"I need a name, Mister."

"I'm Edward Kincaid. I'm a…friend of your sister's and a lieutenant with KCPD."

"Prove it."

More cosmic karma. Stubbornness appeared to be a Masterson family trait.

He patted his waist, but, of course, there was no badge there. "I'm…off duty."

"Well, then you're out of luck. I don't open this door to men I don't know."

"Holly knows me."

There was a pause on the other side of the door. "What's your badge number?"

That much he could give her. "Two-three-one-six. Ask Holly."

"She isn't here right now. Maybe you should come back later."

Not here? A wary tension crept into Edward's muscles. If Holly wasn't at the office, wasn't at home and wasn't answering her cell, then where the heck was she?

"You don't know where Holly is?" No answer. Tension kicked up to outright concern. He rested his hand against the locked door and leaned in, speaking as calmly and concisely as he could. "Jillian? I need you to call Fourth Precinct headquarters." He gave her the number. "Ask anyone there to describe me. You need to let me in."

It took a few minutes of low-pitched talking, but then he heard the chain engage on the door. "Step back a minute," Jillian instructed. The door slid open a crack and a young woman with a dark brown ponytail wearing a Florida Gators sweatshirt peeked through. He unzipped his jacket to show her he wasn't armed, and waited for her to scan him from head to toe. "Dark hair, scars on face, raspy voice. Where's your cane?"

Oh, boy. Another Masterson who needed every detail to have a rational explanation. "Your sister said I didn't need it—that I was only using it as a security blanket."

Jillian screwed her mouth into a contemplative smile. Now that looked familiar. "She likes to fix things, doesn't she."

"Yeah. She was worried about your date with Blake Rivers last night, too."

"Mama Hen talked about that, huh?" He wouldn't say how much. "Then you *do* know her." She closed the door to unhook the chain and then opened it wide. "Come on in."

His first full impression of Jillian Masterson was that she was even taller than her sister, she was healthy and smart and Holly probably worried about her too much. And, she was scared. The darting eyes and tight set to her mouth gave her away.

Edward scanned the apartment's main rooms. Not exactly neat as a pin, with boxes and decorations laid out to prepare for the upcoming holiday. But he couldn't see anything obviously out of place like an open window or ransacked furniture, indicating some kind of break-in. With a nod of permission from Jillian, he moved farther into the apartment, searching the bedrooms and bath as well.

Jillian followed along behind him. "I've been up since seven. When I didn't smell her tea brewing, I got worried. Her bed hasn't even been slept in."

"Have you tried to call her?"

"At work and on her cell. She doesn't answer."

Holly might not have his number identified on her phone, but she'd know her sister's and would answer. If she could.

He didn't bother coming up with logical excuses. He'd caught her sneaking around Caldwell Technologies, getting more deeply involved in his father's murder investigation than he'd ever asked her to. From the trail of dead bodies left in their wake, he knew Z Group was not an organization to be messed with. Plus, she'd been getting those harassing phone calls. If whoever was on the other end of that line had upped his game to a more personal confrontation…

Edward slammed the door shut on all the unspeakable possibilities and headed back to the front door. "I'll make some calls. Is it all right if I post a uniformed officer outside your building? If she turns up, or anything else out of place should happen, I want to know about it ASAP."

Despite the brave set to her chin, Jillian was clearly upset by Holly's disappearance as well. "I've never known her to be in any trouble before. She's the good girl of the family—all I've ever known her to do is work. To stay out all night and not call in just isn't like her."

"I didn't think it would be." He opened the front door, remembering now why he'd given up pursuing any kind of serious relationship with a woman. It hurt too much to worry like this. "Give me your number. I'll call as soon as I know anything."

After exchanging numbers, Jillian caught the door. "Do you think she just had a flat tire or something? It was so cold last night. If she went off the road or couldn't get help…"

If a call to one of his brothers at precinct headquarters didn't turn up an accident report, he'd start calling area hospitals. He shouldn't have let her drive off by herself last night. He should have followed her home instead of calling his sponsor and finding that midnight AA meeting.

Edward swallowed his guilt and his fear and patted Jillian's shoulder. "I'll find her. She'll be just fine. So will you." She nodded, taking more comfort from the words than he did. "Lock your door."

He was at the front door of the building when Jillian came bounding down the stairs after him. "Lieutenant! Lieutenant Kincaid? I found her." She ran up to him, holding her cell phone to her ear, but shaking her head, frowning. "I can hardly understand what she's saying, though."

Edward grabbed the phone from her hand. "Holly?"

"Edward?" She whispered his name on three different breaths. His heart sank. She was crying.

Retribution hit him hard in the gut and he wanted to double over with the pain. "Holly, honey, what's wrong?"

"Help me." Her voice sounded hoarse and weak between sniffles as she tried to control her tears. "It's so hard to breathe. He keeps calling me. I stopped answering my phone. And then I saw Jillian's number."

He hoped that was static from a bad connection and not her phone about to give out. Not Holly about to give out. "Holly?"

"I need air."

"Pull it together, Stick. Where are you? What's wrong?"

Jillian was listening in, her fear rising along with his at the extended silence. "Holly? Talk to us, sis. Please."

When there was no answer, Edward flashed back to the call that had come over his radio two Christmas Eves ago. *Shots fired at your house, Kincaid.*

André Butler sighted in area. Units responding. He closed his eyes and saw his wife and daughter lying in the snow. Saw Butler with his gun standing over them. He couldn't do this again. He couldn't lose anyone else.

His eyes popped open. "Holly!"

"Autopsy." He could barely make out the whispered word. "Please, Edward. Hurry."

"Stay on the line with Jillian, okay, honey? I'm on my way. Stay on the line until I get there." He already had his keys out. He pushed open the door and met a blast of cold air that didn't go as deep as the dreadful chill inside him.

THERE WERE CERTAIN ADVANTAGES to having three brothers who were active-duty cops. When a man needed to speed through the streets of Kansas City without being pulled over, he could call in a favor.

And there wasn't any backup he trusted more than knowing Holden was on the phone, alerting the crime lab's security supervisor to a possible situation in their building and ordering an EMT unit to be on standby at the scene. With Atticus leading the way, lights flashing, and Sawyer closing in behind him, Edward flew toward southern Kansas City and the new crime lab building. The twenty-minute drive took ten.

Ten minutes too long as far as Edward was concerned. Bypassing the parking garage, his SUV fishtailed into the circular drive at the front of the building. Throwing up snow and slush and hopping the curb, his heavy vehicle skidded to a halt outside the main doors.

A news van had somehow joined the race, and pulled in right behind him seconds later. While Edward climbed out of his Jeep, a blond reporter jumped out of the passenger side of the van. Waving to her cameraman to hurry and join her, she ran to catch up with Edward's long, uneven stride. "Excuse me, Detective? It *is* 'detective,' isn't it? I'm Hayley Resnick with the evening news. I cover the crime beat. Don't I recognize you from the André Butler case? You're the cop who killed him with his car."

He fisted his hands and kept walking.

But she moved those legs pretty fast. "Is it true that one of the CSIs has been attacked? Can you tell me what case the attack might be related to?"

"How the hell do you know what's going on here?" He glared down at the microphone she tried to shove in his face. "I just found out about the incident myself."

"Police scanners, detective. I'm allowed to tune in and find out what's going on at KCPD." Her blue eyes sparkled with some kind of triumph. "So there *has* been an incident."

He pushed the microphone away. "Get out of my face."

While Atticus urged him away from the camera light, Sawyer had pulled up in his truck. "Allow me, Ed," he called, running up to join them. "Ms. Resnick. As I recall, you were harassing my wife the last time we met. How's your year been going since then?"

"I owe you one," Edward mouthed.

Sawyer winked. Then he positioned his big, bad self between Edward and the camera, effectively blocking the shot and any more questions from the reporter. "I've got this under control out here." Sawyer's promise was one he could bank on. "I'll get the EMTs inside as soon as they arrive. Keep me posted." Doffing a salute, he turned his attention to making nice with the reporter and her crew while Edward went inside.

"Hey. What's all the fuss? Are you looking for Holly, Lieutenant?" A young man in a white lab coat—the kid with the spiky hair who'd been such a suck-up yesterday in Holly's office—pushed past a pair of waiting security guards.

"Temple, is it?" Edward broke stride long enough to address the CSI. He dared to hope that this was all some kind of mix-up. "Do you know where she is? Have you seen her this morning?"

Either nervous about facing the press himself, or caught up in the excitement of the chaotic scene, Temple's gaze darted from Edward out through the doors and back. "We were supposed to meet for a ballistics briefing a half hour ago, but she never showed."

So much for hope. "Did you try calling her?"

"Uh, yes. At about eight fifteen this morning. Her lab was dark, so I figured she wasn't in yet. I called her cell but she didn't answer."

Edward had left the conversation two sentences ago. He hurried toward the stairwell to the basement, processing the time frame. He'd watch Holly drive away from Caldwell Technologies just after 11 p.m. last night. She'd been out of touch with the world for over ten hours now. And he hadn't been looking for her. He hadn't known she'd even needed him. Son of a… He hadn't done his job.

"Holly!"

He took the stairs two at a time, ignoring the jolts in his knee and ankle each time his foot came down hard on a step. Atticus was thinking a little more rationally, questioning the two guards following them down the stairs. "How much of a search have you gotten done?"

"We located Dr. Masterson's car in the garage. But she never signed in or out of the duty log, sir," one of them reported. "And like Rick said, there was no one in the basement lab when we did a walk-by. We'll have to call in more men to do a room-to-room search."

"Was there any sign of a struggle?"

"No, sir. The cleaning crew went by about three a.m. They said the lab was empty, and everything inside was spic-and-span."

"What about at her car?"

"Not that I could see."

"She's here, A," Edward insisted. "She said *autopsy*."

"I'm not arguing with you. I just want to make sure we have all the facts, in case—"

"In case what?" Edward didn't want to hear the options. He whirled around and glared at his brother. He couldn't handle *in case*.

Atticus, thank God, could keep a cooler head. "Let's just get inside there and do a thorough sweep. I didn't know you and Holly were so close, but I can see how important it is for you to find her. We will."

"Sorry, A." Edward nodded and reached for the door. He wanted to see Holly with his own eyes and put his hands on her and know that she was all right. That she was in one piece. He needed to know that the woman he cared about hadn't been hurt because of him. Again.

He'd deal with the ramifications of *caring* later.

"Whoa." Atticus's hand on his arm stopped Edward from pushing the door handle. He nodded toward the jamb at the base of the door. "Do you see that?"

"See what? Let me in, A." He'd never punched a brother before in his life, not even as kids. But so help him…

But Atticus wouldn't let him pass. "Look."

Tearing his eyes from the lab door, he spared a

second to follow the line of Atticus's pointing finger. He didn't have to ask what his brother was looking at. Edward saw it now, too.

A tiny ruby-red crescent.

He squatted down beside his brother to get a closer look at the tiny shard caught beneath the baseboard beside the door. Even Atticus's keen eye would have overlooked it if it hadn't been painted that Christmas red color.

"Does Holly have manicured nails?" Atticus asked.

All too easily, Edward pictured Holly's long, articulate fingers, sliding into plastic examination gloves or reaching up to gently caress his face. Her nails were sensibly short. Functional. Clear. "No."

"Holden's girlfriend, Liza—when she saw Dad's killer leaving the crime scene at the warehouse, she said she was certain it was a woman." Atticus's gray eyes bored into his. "Could you have stirred something up with your off-the-books investigation? Maybe you're on to something that could lead us to that woman."

And that same woman may have been down here with Holly? "Move!"

Edward shoved himself to his feet and pushed open the door. The wildly desperate feeling that he was already too late tunneled his senses to one purpose—finding Holly. Alive.

Stepping through the doorjamb, he pulled off his leather gloves and used one to flip the switch and flood the lab with light. He was only vaguely aware of Atticus ordering Rick Temple to grab a camera and evidence bag and process the broken nail.

"Are you sure she was here, sir?" The two security guards had followed him in. "It doesn't look like anybody has been in here tonight."

"Please, Edward. Hurry."

"She's here," he said with certainty. Then he walked into her office and saw the chair behind the desk. "She's here."

He picked up two water-stained leather high heels and pushed them into the hands of the young guard who'd doubted him. "She was wearing these last night." He shouted, "Holly?"

"Autopsy."

He looked straight across the room to the glass door with the plain black letters that marked the work she did inside. That marked where Cara and Melinda had rested the night they'd died.

Of all the places in the world to have to look for someone. "Oh, no."

"Ed?"

"In here!" Edward tore across the lab and threw open the door hard enough for it to bounce against the thick glass windows insulating the autopsy room from the rest of the lab. Inside the sterile room he could hear the whirring motors of the cooling and air filtration units.

And he could hear a faint tapping sound.

His eyes zeroed in on the stainless steel gurney wedged beneath the handles on a row of body drawers along the east side of the room. "Holly?"

Tap, tap, tap.

"Help me move this thing."

The tapping grew louder.

With Atticus's help, he shoved the gurney back to the center of the room and they started pulling open each of the body drawers. Empty. Empty.

Tap. Tap.

Empty.

When he felt the weight resistance on the third drawer, Edward nearly cried out. He quickly slid the chamber out of the wall. "Holly?"

A soft gasp answered him. "Help me."

"I'm here, honey. I'm here." Joy soared through him as he glimpsed a cap of dark brown hair, eyes squinting against the bright light, and a cell phone resting against her ear. But relief plummeted down to his toes when he saw all the blood matted in the back of her hair and drying on the tray beneath her head. There was blood on her lab coat, too. And she looked so pale. "Get the EMTs down here!"

"Edward?"

Good. Her eyes hadn't opened but she'd recognized him by sound or mood.

His fingers shook as he brushed the bangs from her forehead. He leaned down to press a kiss to the same spot. Her skin felt clammy, unnaturally cold.

"Where are you hurt? Can you tell me what happened?"

"He hit me…in the head. With a flashlight, I think."

He winced along with her when she tried to roll toward him and moaned. "You have to lie still."

But now she was trying to push herself up. "I want out of here. I'm so cold. I need air. Now."

"The EMTs—"

"No." A tear squeezed between her lashes. "I can't stay in this tomb one more second."

Understanding the desperation in her voice, Edward pried the phone from her hand and handed it off to Atticus. "Introduce yourself to Jillian and tell her I've got her sister." He unzipped his coat and peeled it off, covering Holly's shivering body. "Then bag that phone. I want to know who belongs to every number that's called in."

"Got it."

As Atticus moved to a quiet corner to handle the phone call, Ed slipped his arms beneath Holly's body. "You know about this kind of doctoring, too, right? Can I move you?"

She nodded, and the pain that slight movement caused her knifed through him as well. With her eyes squeezed shut against the ache in her head, she whispered brief instructions about needing to stay warm and stay awake until another professional could examine her. "I can focus my eyes. My head feels like a ton of bricks is shifting around inside it, though."

"I've got you, then." He lifted her, coat and all. "Just stay with me, honey. Stay with me."

Trusting that the head wound and possible shock were the only physical injuries he needed to watch out for, he decided to deal with the emotional and mental injuries caused by the assault. *He* needed to deal with them.

Hugging her against his chest, Edward carried Holly into her office, looking for a bit of privacy as well as the warmth she needed. She didn't weigh enough to put any strain on his mended joints, but still, his legs nearly gave out from tension and worry. Only twenty minutes had passed since Jillian had received Holly's call, but he felt drained, as though he'd been worrying about this woman's welfare for a lifetime.

Before his willpower failed him, Edward kicked the chair out from under her desk and sank into it, spilling Holly into his lap.

"No," she protested, curling her fingers into the front of his sweater and trying to hold on. "Please. I don't want to be alone. I couldn't get out, and he kept calling me, over and over, and there was no one…"

"Shh, I'm not letting go. I just need to warm you up." He allowed the distance between them just long enough to wrap his coat more securely around her before drawing her back into his arms. "He's not going to hurt you again. Do you understand? I'm not going to let him hurt you."

Tucking her head beneath his chin, Holly curled herself into a ball and burrowed against him. She needed to talk about it, to get the horrible experience out of her, and though it angered him to hear about the shadow and the lights going out and the flashlight crashing down on the back of her skull, Edward listened. He clenched his jaw and held his curse as she described the sensation of waking inside what was virtually a steel coffin. When she described the tormenting calls that kept her from answering her phone or calling someone until she began to get disoriented from the mix of what was probably a concussion and a shrinking supply of oxygen, he rubbed his hands up and down her arms and along the length of her legs. He needed to generate some heat into her chilled body and reassure himself that beyond bumps and abrasions and the clotted gash behind her left ear, she truly was in one piece.

Edward pressed his lips to the crown of her hair. He'd reached her in time. He hadn't failed her. Holly hadn't died like his wife and daughter had.

"You scared me, Stick. I couldn't find you and I thought…" An unforgiving fist squeezed his heart.

Maybe sensing the depth of his distress, Holly released her death grip on his sweater and wound her arms around his neck, tilting her face up to his. "It's okay, Edward. I'll be okay."

She touched her lips to his. Something hard and

anguished unfurled inside him at that gentle caress. Palming the back of her neck, he lifted her higher and claimed her mouth in a ragged, needy, possessive kiss. The bulk of his coat was too much between them and he slid his arm inside, catching her tight against his chest, palming her hip and stroking her back.

She speared her fingers into his hair and hugged his shoulders, giving him everything he needed to make the raw hurt inside him go away. "Shh. I'm okay." She kissed his eyes, cradled his face between her hands, kissed him again. "You're not responsible for what happened. It's not your fault."

She was the victim here. And yet she was the one comforting him?

Though he couldn't deny how much he craved her tenderness, he eased his hold on her and settled her back in his lap. "I'm sorry, honey. I'm so sorry you got hurt."

"Thank you for finding me."

"Thank you for living," he whispered against her hair, hugging her almost painfully tight. She tucked her head beneath his chin and snuggled close as he covered her again with his coat.

"I'll be fine now," she promised, whispering against his beating heart. "Just don't let go."

It took both Atticus and Sawyer to pry her from his arms to allow the EMTs to clean and stitch the wound in her scalp.

By the time they'd dismissed her and she'd given an official statement to Atticus, Holly was clear eyed and able to stand on her own two feet. She still wore Edward's fleece-lined coat around her shoulders as she led Atticus through the crime scene.

"Be sure they process the trace from under my fingernails. It may just be from my own struggles in the morgue unit, but I could have gotten something off my attacker."

"I'll have the lab look at the debris the medics removed from your head wound as well."

Holly nodded. "There were tissue samples on the cart I knocked over. I don't see any of the containers now, but I catalogued them in the computer so trace will know what to exclude."

Atticus followed Holly toward the autopsy room, asking questions and jotting answers. "Could you tell whether your attacker was male or female?"

"I suppose it could have been a woman. She wasn't any taller than I was. I think he or she tried to pick me up but ended up dragging me."

"Maybe you injured her in the struggle," A suggested.

Holly pulled the coat more tightly around her as they entered the air-conditioned autopsy room. "The lights went out and he—or she—was dressed all in black. I smacked him with my clipboard, but I couldn't see the face. Once he hit me, everything got fuzzy. I passed out and woke up in—"

The door closed behind them, leaving Edward to watch without hearing any more of the violent report. Holly described everything so coolly, so practically, but he was pretty much a mess of irrational rage and gut-deep fear.

He didn't know how long Sawyer had been standing beside him until his brother made a few observations of his own. "If the cleaning crew was here between two and three, then that fingernail you found had to be deposited after three. Is that when we're placing the attack?"

Edward nodded, forcing his brain to think analytically about the details of Holly's assault instead of focusing on the stitches and bandage that interfered with the way her short, sleek haircut normally fell into place. He needed to listen to what his brothers were saying with an unbiased ear instead of coloring his opinions through the pale cast to Holly's cheeks.

"Does this place look too clean to you?" he asked.

Sawyer shrugged. "It's a sterile lab."

"Yeah, but if the cleaning crew was here *before* the attack—"

"—then her attacker cleaned up. Do you think he or she was after something in the lab and Holly just happened to be in the way?"

"I think the attacker took what Holly was working on. There are no evidence bags, no samples, no notes." Edward scraped his palm over the scarred ridges and angles of his jaw. "Can I make a confession to you? As a brother, not a cop."

"I'm listening."

"Holly and I 'borrowed' something from Caldwell Technologies last night."

"Bill's company? Mom was hosting the party with him, wasn't she?"

"Yeah." It felt awkward to be discussing the man whom Edward and his brothers had camped and fished with growing up, a man who'd been as close as a brother to their father, as if he was some kind of suspect. "We located a stash of disintegrator bullets."

Like the ones three prison escapees—and suspected Z Group employees—had used during a crime spree earlier in the year. Sawyer had become personally involved in that case when he discovered that his wife's abusive ex-husband was one of the escaped convicts. "Are you saying they're the same kind of trademark bullet Z Group uses?"

"It's possible. And there were a lot of them—not a single prototype like Bill told us when we questioned him a couple of months ago."

"You think Bill's a part of this?"

Sawyer's incredulity matched his own. "He and Dad served together in military intelligence years ago. They were both a part of Z Group, too, before the government shut down their operation in Sarajevo. Dad's journals—the ones Atticus and

Brooke found—said that Dad had discovered Z Group was still in operation, trading arms and technology on the underground market. Maybe Dad ran across something like this at Bill's company, too. Maybe that's how he knew the organization had never died."

"No way could Bill be involved with Dad's murder. He's family." Sawyer's emotions ran pretty close to the surface. "No way. Mom's been dating him. Just because his company produces something similar to the disintegrators doesn't mean he's supplying Z Group with weapons or that he's any part of their cover-up."

"Down, boy." He wanted to agree with Sawyer's defense of the man who had always been a second father to them. But facts didn't lie. "I'm not accusing Bill of anything. But either he knows about the production of that ammunition, or he has a traitor in his company who's been using him."

"One of those bullets nearly killed my son," Sawyer spoke on a low, tense voice. "Bill wouldn't let that happen. Dad wouldn't have let Bill get involved with something like that. If he had anything to do with Z Group, Dad would have stopped him. Too many people have died."

At this bleak moment of clarity, Edward didn't feel just like the older brother—he felt ancient. "Dad *did* try to stop them. That's why he's dead."

They stood together in silence while each man

processed the possibilities. Sawyer was calmer when he spoke again. "So Dad found out something illegal was going on at Caldwell Technologies. And either Bill's involved, or Bill is in danger because of it." He glanced down at Edward. "So, how do we find out exactly what Dad discovered? How do we prove Bill's innocence or guilt?"

"First, we prove those are the same disintegrators Z Group uses. Then we find out who's using the company to make them."

Sawyer nodded. "And knowing who's behind the bullets can lead us to Dad's killer."

"Right."   ·

"Do you have a plan as to how we can get a hold of one of those bullets legally?"

"I'm working on it." It might come down to confronting Bill himself. But Edward was keeping his options open. "Holly was going to run some tests to compare what we found to bullets she's removed during autopsies. I just didn't know she was going to do it last night—while she was here alone."

Though he couldn't hear what she was saying, he could see Holly through the glass windows, clutching his coat around her shoulders yet standing up straight and pointing out information to Atticus. How the hell could she keep it together like that and function as a professional? Where did she get that kind of strength?

Sawyer's elbow butted against his arm, nudging

him from his thoughts. "You've got it bad for her, don't you, bro."

No. He couldn't. "I don't want to 'have it bad' for anybody."

"I don't think we get to choose who gets inside us, Ed. It just happens. And you either seize the gift that's there and fight for it with everything you have—or you waste it."

"When did you become the family philosopher?"

"The day I followed my big brother's example and married the woman I love." Sawyer pulled back his sleeve and checked his watch. "Speaking of… I need to get to an OB/GYN appointment with Mel." Sawyer's wife of eight months was five months pregnant with their second child. Their first child was Sawyer's adopted son from Melissa's first marriage.

"We're cool. Go. I'll call you if I need something."

"You better. Hey, are we going to see you Christmas Eve at Mom's? You know she wants us all there."

"I thought you were leaving."

"I'm going. Promise you'll think about Christmas Eve, though. We're keeping it low-key, just family." Sawyer paused for one last friendly shot. "And Ed? Looks to me like this investigation is getting more and more dangerous. Maybe you ought to think about strapping on your gun and wearing your badge again."

After Sawyer left, Edward felt an uneasy pang of

envy for the second-eldest in his family as he looked forward to the birth of a child with the woman he loved. Except for the veil of their father's unsolved murder hanging over him, Sawyer's life had fallen into place. He had a wife, love, children, marriage. He was a good detective and a better man.

Edward had once been in that same place. How could he stand to know that kind of happiness again—knowing exactly what it would be like to lose it all?

Where did he find strength like Sawyer's? Or Atticus's? Or even baby brother Holden's?

Where did he find that kind of strength?

"Call me if there are any more questions I can answer." Holly opened the autopsy room door ahead of Atticus and reentered the lab. Then, still hugging Edward's coat around her shoulders, a smile blossomed across her pale lips. A smile for him. "Please tell me you're still here because you're waiting to take me home."

Edward nodded. "I'll give you a ride home, Stick."

"A ride?" Her smile dimmed. "You won't be staying?"

"I don't know that I'd be good company today. Besides, you need your rest."

Her eyes narrowed as if she was assessing him under a microscope. But then she nodded and moved past him into her office. "I'll get my things."

He might just be able to summon the strength to

leave her with a guard and her sister, and walk away once he knew she was safely tucked into bed.

But he didn't know if he'd have the strength to stay.

Chapter Eight

He found her in the bathroom of her hotel suite, with a white, fuzzy robe strategically draped over skin that was still damp from her shower. She sat on the toilet seat with her legs propped up on the edge of the tub. And she was painting her fingernails as if she was getting ready for a Christmas party, not the confrontation he expected from an emergency summons like this one.

He had an idea that, no matter how hot the water ran from the faucet, nothing but ice would ever run through this woman's veins.

"Did you get it?" he asked, loosening his tie and unbuttoning his collar.

"I have it right here." She dug beneath a badge and chain and the other trophies she'd collected and pulled a small clear plastic bag from the trinket box beside her. She tossed the bag to him.

"Looks like one of mine," he confirmed. He held the bag up to the bright lights of the vanity. The surface of the bullet inside the bag was uneven, as if parts of it had been chipped away, fracturing the cohesive elements that held the casing together in its cylindrical shape. "It looks as though Dr. Masterson ran some tests on it."

"Don't worry. I destroyed her research notes as well as all of the vials she'd been working with." She held her hand up in front of her and splayed her fingers, frowning as she inspected her handiwork. Then she squeezed out a dollop of scented hand cream and rubbed it into her skin. "I do hate having to wear gloves all the time. My skin is cracking from all the sanitizing I had to do this evening. And your winters here in Missouri wreck my hands."

This would be the perfect opportunity to reintroduce his idea about retiring from the business and setting up a permanent vacation home on some tropical island together. Only, the thought of spending the rest of his life with this woman no longer held the appeal for him it once had.

Oh, there was something shamefully irresistible about the way she displayed her body for him. His lust for her bombshell figure and bold lovemaking would probably never abate. And he'd never had any complaints about the insane amount of money she'd made since their partnership had begun.

But this evening, watching her primp and pamper herself while an exclusive Hayley Resnick news story about a vicious attack on one of KCPD's local criminalists played on the early evening news, he truly understood how ruthless this woman could be. Relaxing his guard around her would be a bad idea. Believing that she would ever put his needs or wishes above her own would be a stupid one.

"Did you kill her when you retrieved the bullet?"

"Didn't have to." She blew on her nails. "She never saw me, and I left a very tidy crime scene behind me.

"However…" She capped the tube of hand cream and stood, tying the front of her robe together as she approached. "I'd like to know who the incompetent was who allowed that woman to get her hands on one of your inventions in the first place." She walked right up to him, sliding her body against his. "I want that person eliminated."

Lust and contempt crawled in equal parts through his body. "What if I told you *I* was responsible for the lapse in security that allowed Kincaid and his doctor girlfriend to get their hands on a disintegrating bullet? Would you believe me?"

"Were you?" She smiled at the idea. "That's awfully nostalgic of you, dear. Seems I remember a time in the past when you played both sides of the fence, too." She walked her newly painted fingers up his chest and tapped his lips. "Everyone in Z Group believed that Irina Zorinsky Hansford was the double agent. They even plotted to kill her to eliminate the danger she posed to all of their operatives in the field. But *you* were the double agent, weren't you, dear. No one but me has ever known that truth, have they?"

It was a fact she never let him forget. Keeping *his* secret all this time meant that he had to keep hers, as well. And do her bidding, no matter how the taste for this kind of work had grown bitter over the years.

"I'll move the remaining supply out with one of the European shipments tonight. If KCPD comes back with a warrant to seize another sample, I can claim plausible deniability." Her penchant for using the untraceable bullets to complete her handiwork with a gun made it imperative that the police never make the connection between Irina's staged murder and Caldwell Technologies' link to Z Group. "Will that suffice?"

"For now. But even the fact that you would joke about giving information to the Kincaids concerns me. It makes me wonder exactly which side of the game you're playing. You're not letting your interest in the wholesome Widow Kincaid affect your loyalty to me, are you?" She trailed one red-tipped nail around the edge of his collar. For such a beautiful woman, the skin on her hands—with their scratches and patches of red, irritated skin—really did show the hazards of her trade. "Her noble, departed John will always come first for her. You understand that, don't you, dear?"

Perhaps if this woman had ever shown him real love beyond their intense physical compatibility, he might not be having second thoughts about their alliance. He sifted his fingers through the long, curling locks of her hair. "And the money will always come first for you, yes?"

"I don't want to give up the money any more than you want to go to prison. That's the way it has always worked between us. And if there is any problem that arises—be it a nosy detective or an employee who threatens to talk about the operation or you having second thoughts about our arrangement—I either hire someone to deal with it, or I take care of it myself." She untied her robe and let it slide off of her naked body. Whatever was left of his conscience was doomed as she stretched up to kiss him. "So don't become a problem, dear."

"LOOK. I FOUND THE ONES WE made when we were kids."

"Mom kept everything, didn't she?" Holly cradled a cup of tea between her palms, trying to keep her focus on Jillian's tree-decorating adventure, and not on the gravel-voiced detective who was pacing back and forth in her kitchen.

Edward had spent the night on the very couch where she was sitting now, never complaining about the discomfort of a bed that was too short, never saying much of anything beyond the perfunctory

"This will do" to the blankets and pillow she'd brought him last night and the *"Thanks"* to the coffee she'd served him this morning.

It was as if the closeness she'd felt when he'd pulled her out of the morgue bin yesterday had never happened. She'd seen a savior. Warmth. Security. For the hours immediately following her rescue, Edward Kincaid had been a solid rock she could cling to. She'd been so afraid, practically losing her mind with a newly discovered claustrophobia and the cruel torment of the ringing phone.

But then Edward was there. His husky voice comforted her as no other sound could. His arms had given her a chance to surrender her survival armor long enough that she could begin to calm and heal inside. A glance from those gray eyes across the lab reminded her that she wasn't alone. A steady hand to hold while the EMT had cleaned and sutured her scalp had made the pain bearable.

A kiss had made her feel she was loved.

But the man who'd driven her back to her apartment and promised to stay until a new guard could be posted outside her building was a far different man than the one who'd rescued her, shielded her and loved her.

The detective in her kitchen needed a shave, some fresh clothes, and a swift kick in the pants.

Didn't he realize that she wanted him here? That she would have welcomed him in her bed to hold her through the night or at her breakfast table to share a conversation, or on the couch beside her, just to be near him? She supposed this professional distance he insisted upon was due in some small part to the fact they had a chaperone in Jillian staying with her over the holidays. But she sensed that something far more complex than propriety had turned him into the cold-eyed watchdog stalking through her apartment.

He was already on his third phone call this morning, and it wasn't even eight o'clock. "Yeah, I can be there for the briefing," he promised someone. "But I may be running late. I have to make a stop first. One of my informants thinks he's on to something. No, I don't need backup for..."

"Hello? Earth to Holly." Jillian's amused voice finally registered after Edward disappeared into the kitchen again.

She set her tea on the lamp table beside the couch and turned back to her sister. "I'm sorry. What did you say?"

"I was asking what you think." Jillian gestured to the tree behind her where she'd been hanging the ornaments from the boxes Holly was opening for her. "I'm grouping the ornaments into themes this year. Angels near the top. Reindeer in the middle. And Santas on the bottom near where the presents will be."

Holly summoned a halfhearted smile. Jillian was trying hard to be the big sister here—giving her a sedentary job that allowed her to rest for the day, entertaining her with family stories about the ornaments as she hung them on the tree and distracting her from Edward's cold shoulder.

She did her best to play along. She pointed out a hole where Jillian could hang another Santa and teased her. "So, you think you're getting presents?"

"Please," Jillian scoffed. "I've seen your closet. Either you're planning on decorating a Plaza storefront window or you've been shopping. I'm figuring at least one or two boxes out of that stack is for me."

"Snoop."

"Shopaholic."

"Stick?"

Holly nearly sprang up off the couch at the sound of Edward's voice behind her.

He held up a hand, apologizing for the start and telling her to stay put. She stood up anyway, glad her vision had stopped spinning with every sudden movement this morning. "You're leaving?"

He'd pulled his coat off the back of her dining room chair and was shrugging into it. She circled the couch, hoping to glimpse some hint of regret in his eyes. But all she saw was cold, efficient cop.

Edward buttoned his coat as he walked to the door. "I need to run an errand, and then I'm meeting with Kevin Grove, the detective who's heading up the investigation into Dad's murder."

"I know Kevin." She followed him. Despite her

confusion over the relationship signals Edward was sending, her own investigative curiosity kicked in. "Has there been a new development? Do you think my attack is related to your father's murder?"

"I can't say for sure. But Grove is bringing in Bill Caldwell and Blake Rivers for questioning— nothing official—and he's hoping they can share enough data about the disintegrator bullets they developed to justify seizing one as *legal* evidence." He pulled his leather gloves from his pockets and slipped them on. "Grove wants me there as a consultant to see if I can talk Bill into cooperating. Otherwise, we probably don't have enough grounds for a search warrant."

Holly held the door when he opened it, wishing she'd been invited to that meeting as well. "Even if my attacker took all my notes and samples, my memory works just fine. That bullet dissolved into nothing when I combined it with human blood. I've never seen anything else like it. If it's not the same make of ammo I pulled out of your father and the other victims, then I'll surrender my M.E.'s license. Someone at Caldwell Technologies is working for Z Group—and killing off anyone who can connect them to it."

Her certainty seemed to finally break through his stoic facade. He paused in the hallway and turned with a nod. "I know you're right. In my gut, I feel it. But neither my gut nor your experiments will make our case. I need to find another way to trip up Z Group."

"Is there anything I can do to help?"

He reached out and cupped the side of her neck, stroking his thumb along her jaw. Relief and reassurance swelled inside her and she turned her cheek into the soft leather and firm hand. "Just stay safe," he whispered, in that growly timbre she craved. "There's a patrolman in a car outside. If you go anywhere, he goes with you."

Holly nodded her understanding.

"Remember, the E.R. doctor who double-checked you last night said you should take it easy today." He inclined his head toward her doorway. "Relax and spend time with your sister and concentrate on the tree and getting ready for..." He just couldn't say the word, could he? He fixed a smile on his lips for her benefit. "Decorate to your heart's content, okay? Temple has the tests under control at the lab and I'm doing some legwork. I'll call you as soon as I find out anything."

"Thanks for keeping me in the loop." *At least.*

He leaned in and kissed her cheek in a tender, unsatisfying, awkward goodbye. As he released her, she reached out and fastened the top button of his coat. She turned up the collar to keep him warm and then tugged him close.

The kiss she gave him was brief and hot and shameless, offering everything she felt inside.

Pulling away, he gave her a slight nod. Meaning what? He understood how deeply she cared? He agreed that things had gotten decidedly complicated between them yesterday, and uncomfortably awkward for them this morning? Or maybe it was just a twitch and he didn't understand anything about what was happening between them at all.

Holly retreated into her apartment, and he pulled the door closed behind her. "Lock up," he ordered.

She didn't hear him walk away until she had both the chain and dead bolt in place.

"He's a barrel of laughs today, isn't he?" Jillian appeared from behind the tree, adjusting a spiral of garland to make room for another ornament. "I can't tell if he's gone all Terminator on us because he thinks he has to do that in order to protect you, or if he's just not a morning person."

"He was pretty distant last night, too," Holly pointed out, reluctantly dismissing the morning person theory. There was something eating at Edward from the inside out. But since he wouldn't talk and she couldn't read minds, she could only guess at what had put him into such diehard cop mode.

She picked up the folded blankets he'd used and carried them to the linen closet between the two bedrooms. His familiar masculine scent lingered in the wool, warming and saddening her at the same time. She was falling in love with the gruff, flawed, complex man. And on some level, she knew he cared about her. The clues were there in the way he touched her and kissed her and insisted she be safe. It was almost as though his feelings were there for her, too. But he couldn't—or wouldn't—act on them for some noble or fearful or completely selfish reason.

He claimed he wasn't a cop anymore, but his actions showed that he was, through and through.

Once he admitted that truth to himself and the world, then maybe it would be easier for him to admit that his heart was still in good working order. After the tragedies he'd endured, he was entitled to be cautious about caring again. He might have a limp, he could still walk. Even without his cane. He might be wounded inside, but he could still love.

She couldn't be more certain of that conclusion than if she had the science to prove it.

Science. A thought blipped through her mind as she put away the blankets. Proof. She strolled back to the living room, shuffling through a record of vague impressions, searching for something that should have registered sooner. "Tests."

"Temple has the tests under control at the lab."

"Now what do you suppose he meant by that?"

"Uh-oh. Nancy Drew alert." Jillian crossed her arms in front of her, grinning. "What did you think of?"

There was nothing vague running through her mind now. She was working three steps ahead, putting thought into action.

She brushed her hair behind her ears, carefully checking for signs of anything more than superficial discomfort from her stitched-up wound. "May I borrow your phone?"

Jillian glanced at the one sitting right beside her on the lamp table. "Um. Sure. Here." She pulled her cell from the pocket of her jeans.

Holly clasped the phone between her hands, then headed for the closet to pull out her short pink coat. "I mean, is it okay if I take this with me? You said you'd be at home all day decorating the place—can you get by with using the land line?"

"Of course. But, wait, where are you going? Edward said you should take it easy today."

"I'll take it easy at work." She carefully pulled her stocking cap down over her hair and wrapped her scarf around her neck. "I'll ask the patrolman downstairs to give me a lift to the lab since my car's there, anyway. And I'll make sure he calls someone to come watch our building."

"I'm not worried about me." Jillian hustled around her to block the door. "I'm worried about you."

"Don't be." Holly smiled and squeezed Jillian's hand. "Everyone keeps telling me to take it easy. But I can't really relax until I find the answers I need. And I think I know where to find them."

She hugged her sister and hurried downstairs to the front door, pausing to punch in Rick's number before heading out into the cold, sunny air. "Rick?

Yeah, it's Holly. I'm coming into the office—would you have time to do a consult with me?"

Her attacker hadn't stolen *all* of her work last night.

Now she just had to make nice with Rick Temple until she could get the print-out she'd left for him out of his desk.

EDWARD WATCHED HIS OLD FRIEND Jamal down his third hot dog and wondered how a man who'd lived most of his adult life on the streets of No-Man's-Land, KCPD's nickname for one of the area's most troubled neighborhoods, could still have such enthusiasm for life.

"Yes, I definitely think the chili cheese is the best." He wiped sauce from the corner of his mouth with the end of his sleeve, yet spoke like he was reviewing a four-star restaurant. "Though the mustard and sauerkraut dog kicked up the flavor quite a bit."

For the price of a three-course lunch from a hot dog stand, Jamal had agreed to meet Edward in Washington Park and share the latest news he'd gleaned. Edward stamped his feet on the brick walking path until Jamal had adjusted his cap and earmuffs atop his bald head and pulled down his sleeves-cum-napkin over his bare fingers. Gloves would be the next form of payment he'd offer the septuagenarian, whether today's information panned out or not.

When Jamal moved out, Edward shortened his stride to match. "So, buddy, what do you have for me? On the phone this morning you said you had heard something about my brothers?"

"Not your brothers, my friend. You."

"Somebody's talking about Edward Kincaid on the streets?"

"You're the man who killed André Butler, ain't you?" Edward scanned back and forth across the park area, wondering where all these *somebodies* were who thought his hell and retribution made for an interesting topic of conversation. Except for the statue of George Washington himself, the place was deserted. Jamal continued with a world-weary shrug, "André was no good. Turned his back on everything his mama tried to teach him."

No way was he going to take a trip down *that* memory lane today. "Is that all you've got for me? People reminiscing about getting Butler off the streets?"

"Nope. Nope." Jamal climbed over a drift to the sidewalk that led down toward the barbershop where Edward had picked him up a half hour earlier. "What I'm hearin' is that you are on a righteous path again."

"Righteous?" Edward shook his head, carefully stepping over the same drift. "Who's saying I'm gunning for them?"

"Not who. What. I've got sources talkin' about what you want. That you're gettin' close, stirring up the order of things the way you did when you arrested André and his boys."

Had he been off the streets so long that he couldn't follow Jamal's slang anymore? Or was the old man babbling just to get some food in his belly? "I said I wanted to find one of those Z rings."

"Yes. Se-rill-ik." Jamal sounded out the word phonetically and grinned. "I looked it up in the shelter library. It looks like a number three."

"Yeah. We had this conversation before." Edward was already late for the meeting with Kevin Grove and his brothers. He'd left Holly with a rookie guard watching over her. He couldn't afford to be wasting his time here if Jamal didn't start making sense. He swallowed hard to keep the bite out of his voice. "You didn't find one of those rings for me, did you?"

"Nope."

Jamal stopped. Edward caught himself a step later and turned. His old friend from the streets was grinning from ear to ear. "What?"

"I didn't find no ring. But I found a Cyrillic Z."

Edward didn't want to burst his friend's proud bubble. "In the encyclopedia where you looked it up?"

Jamal arched a scraggly brow and shook his head as though Edward was the fool. "On a woman's wrist. Least I heard tell about it. A man I know works for the city. He's a sanitation engineer—"

"Jamal!"

His friend pulled his stained sleeve back from his hand and pointed to the inside of his wrist. "Freddie said he met a woman with a tattoo right here. A teeny, tiny number three inside a circle. A Cyrillic Z."

Edward nearly hugged his skinny friend. "Please tell me it wasn't on a body inside his truck."

"Freddie was doing dumpster pickup in the alleys last night. He caught a woman—nice-lookin' older gal, he said, with long dark hair—though she wasn't dressed nice—throwing somethin' out in one of the dumpsters. She gave him a hundred dollars and said to forget he ever saw her." Jamal sensed Edward's next question. "When she reached up with the money, he saw the tattoo." Jamal laughed. "He thought it was fake."

"The tattoo?"

"The hundred."

Edward could barely keep his feet planted. But he needed to make sure that this was the break he and his brothers had been waiting for. "Did Freddie happen to see what she dumped in the trash?"

Jamal nodded. "He showed it to me when he flashed me the hundred dollar bill. Broken glass and bottles and stuff. She was probably dumpin' her drugs."

Or evidence stolen from a crime lab.

Edward linked his hand beneath Jamal's elbow and hurried toward the warmth of the barbershop. "Can you introduce me to Freddie?"

"Sure. You ain't takin' his hundred dollars, are

you? I know you cops take things for a case and they don't always come back. But Freddie's earned—"

"I'll trade with him, I promise." He paused to open the door for Jamal. "And Freddie's sure it was a Cyrillic Z?"

"You bet. Because I told him and all my friends that you was lookin' for one." That's why his name was on the streets. "You got rid of André for us, and good folks are lookin' to repay the favor. If Edward Kincaid wants a Cyrillic Z, we'll find him one."

Edward smiled. "Now that's righteous."

"THINK OF IT LIKE A MODERN version of the Minié balls developed during the Civil War." Rick Temple drew slashing lines exiting the crude rifle he'd already drawn on the white board in his office. "They expanded as they traveled through the grooves of the rifle, increasing their range and power, but also beginning their decomp."

"Rick, I just need the print-out back. Not an entire history lesson. I still need to stop by Trace and DNA before I head out." Holly held out her hand, but he ignored her request and kept on drawing. This was like some kind of tedious video game where she had to complete the entire task before she could move on to the next level. Conceding to the rules of Rick's ego, Holly pulled her hand back to the strap of her purse. Apparently, she wasn't getting that piece of paper or the lab reports from her attack until she'd heard the lecture through to its very end. "I thought that Minié balls were made of iron."

"They were." Now Rick was writing out a chemical formula. "Iron rusts and breaks down when exposed to the elements or during long-term exposure to the moisture inside the human body. There are records from the war about veterans who weren't killed outright when they were shot. But the projectile lodged in their body where it began to decompose, and then years later they died of the toxins released by the foreign object in their system." She didn't dare interrupt him to say that she read history books, too. "Our disintegrators work in basically the same way, but at a greatly accelerated rate. Of course, the impact seems to kill people outright."

"So your theory is that if any of the victims had survived their wounds—"

"—then most likely they'd die from the decomposing toxins in their systems." Rick finally put the print-out back in its envelope. "Those bullets are deadly in more ways then one. Can you imagine the havoc it would wreak on a population where medical care is minimal?"

"Let's hope we never have to find out." Holly fixed a smile on her face as he turned around and handed her the information she'd asked for ten minutes ago. "Thanks, Rick. It's good to know I have someone so smart and thorough working on my team."

Pleased with himself and his report, she supposed, Rick held on to the envelope, blocking her exit and making sure he had her attention. "Don't you want to know about the other tests?"

With a slight tug, the print-out was hers. She stuffed the envelope into her purse and slung it over her shoulder. "I'm on my way to Trace now."

"Well, let me save you the trip." He circled his desk and picked up a pair of file folders from his in-box. "Lieutenant Kincaid and his brother Atticus asked me to run some tests regarding your attack."

"They asked *you?*"

There he was in front of her again. "Well, I've been running things since you got hurt."

Holly didn't have to tilt her chin to look him in the eye. "I've only been gone one day."

Rick rested his hip against the corner of his desk and sat back. His arms brushed against hers, and Holly flinched. "You know, I enjoy working with you, side by side like this, rather than taking orders from you. Ever since you got your promotion to team leader, you hide yourself down in your lab. It's almost as though you're keeping secrets from us." He winked and leaned closer to share a conspiratorial whisper. "It's like you don't trust us."

Holly pushed him out of her personal space, annoyed and frankly a little uncomfortable with this side of Rick's personality. "I prefer to work alone. That's nothing new. I concentrate better in the lab that way."

"It just feels unfriendly to me. And I think we could be good friends, Holly, if you gave us a chance. We could, you know, look out for each other—so that maybe something like what happened to you in the lab doesn't happen again."

Was that why he took such delight in playing his practical jokes on her? Through some adolescent sense of logic, was that how Rick was trying to draw her out of her reserved shell to become more like one of the gang? "I didn't know you felt that way. I'll try to do better and be more…social."

"Asking me for help with your chemical composite print-out was a good start."

Ugh. They weren't in junior high and Holly didn't need the figurative pat on the head. She snatched the files from Rick's hand. "Could I just see the results from Trace and DNA now?"

She turned her back on him and opened up the first report, detailing the scrapings taken from beneath her fingernails. "Epithelial," she read aloud. Skin. From her attacker, she hoped. Holly quickly opened the second file for the DNA results. "Female." Her attacker *had* been a woman. Like the Kincaid brothers had suggested. Female like the woman who'd murdered their father. And yet: "No hits in CODIS." No direct match. Whoever had attacked her hadn't ever been arrested for any kind of felony.

Rick tapped the folder she'd been reading from. "Did you notice this?"

Holly scanned the paragraph at the end of the page. "A familial connection?"

"We found two links in the system, in fact," Rick pointed out, seeming pleased to do so. "Though the DNA strands didn't positively identify the woman donor, we did find a relative in the police staff records. The other is in the deceased databank. Brooke Hansford and Tony Fierro." Holly knew Brooke as Atticus Kincaid's fiancée, and administrative assistant to Major Mitch Taylor, who ran the Fourth Precinct. She knew Anthony Fierro as a dead body in her autopsy room. Tattooed from head to toe—including one tiny Cyrillic *Z* like the mark she'd found on all of Z Group's former operatives—Fierro had been found murdered in his jail cell shortly after attacking Brooke. And now it looked like Brooke was his sister? "Eeuw."

"Ah. I see you got to the part about Brooke Hansford and Tony Fierro sharing a biological mother." Rick seemed so happy with himself to have figured out more than Holly had, that she simply let him tell her the answers. "The DNA sample taken from your fingertips also matches the nail chip recovered from just outside your lab. They're from the same woman."

"Who is…?"

"Another deceased."

"Impossible. The woman who knocked me out and left me to die was very much alive."

Rick shrugged. "The DNA matches a woman in military intelligence's deceased file."

"Give me a name, Rick."

"Irina Zorinsky Hansford."

Irina Zorinsky? Holly knew that name. Though any mention of her had been conveniently deleted from her files when her computer had been hacked back in April, Edward had talked about her. John Kincaid had written about Irina Zorinsky in his journals.

"Thanks." Rick Temple may not have run the actual lab tests, but suddenly, he seemed a lot less annoying now that he'd reported the DNA results to her. She patted Rick on the shoulder and smiled. "Thank you."

He raised his hand to briefly cover hers. "You're welcome."

Holly pulled away and hurried out the door without another word. As she strode quickly down the hall toward the elevators, she drew Jillian's phone from her purse and punched in Edward's number. Irina Zorinsky Hansford had been one of Z Group's original operatives, according to John Kincaid. An eyewitness report put a woman at the scene of John's murder, a woman who'd stolen a souvenir from around John Kincaid's neck.

"Come on, Edward, pick up." She needed to verify information from his father's journals. She wanted to discuss possibilities. She settled for leaving a voice mail and urged him to track her down because she just might have found the break they'd been looking for.

A woman had attacked Holly and stolen the bullet and test results that might very well provide answers to John's murder. Could John's killer be the same woman? Could she be Irina Zorinsky Hansford?

But Irina was listed in the deceased file.

Think, Holly. Figure it out.

But the impossible couldn't make logical sense. "How did a dead woman wind up in my lab if I wasn't doing an autopsy on her?"

Chapter Nine

The bustling detectives' floor of the Fourth Precinct building sounded familiar, with its drone of conversations, punctuated by an occasional laugh or raised voice. It smelled familiar, with its oddly aromatic mix of twenty-four hour coffee, lemony cleansers and polishes and a rare note of off-the-street funk or high-class cologne.

It felt familiar to be standing in the observation room, looking through a one-way mirror, watching Kevin Grove as the bulldog-faced detective asked pretty boy Blake Rivers some tough questions.

But Edward wasn't sure that *familiar* meant he was ready for *comfortable* or *right*. It probably felt pretty familiar for a repeat offender to have a pair of handcuffs slapped on his wrists, too.

And if one more person said, "Welcome back" or "Great to see you," followed by an apologetic, "Oh. I thought...well, it was good to see you, anyway," when they saw his visitor's badge, Edward was going to ram his fist through the mirrored glass. He didn't know what got him the most: the idea that a few of his former coworkers seemed to think he was some kind of legendary department hero who deserved to be put up on a pedestal, or the fact that others thought he was a hero of the fallen kind, who needed folks tiptoeing around him while speaking in sympathetic whispers.

All he was certain of was that from the moment he'd entered the building for the first time in two years, an uneasy wariness had been crawling beneath his skin. The precinct commander, Major Mitch Taylor, hadn't wasted any time calling him into his office.

"Now that you've passed the physical, Kincaid, I can't keep you on medical leave. I want you back—if your head's going to be in the game. I can use a good man with the experience you have on my team." Major Taylor made it seem like the choices were black-and-white. "So, are you turning in your gun and badge and taking the pension? Or should I expect to see you sitting at your desk on January second?"

"Two weeks?"

"And counting." The big, barrel-chested boss man circled his desk with an outstretched hand. "You know where I stand. But it's your decision."

Edward shook his hand, thanking him for his support, promising to think hard on his future career at KCPD. Then he went and joined his brothers in the observation room.

Knowing that KCPD's raid on Caldwell Technologies had been a bust didn't help convince him he was ready to be a working cop again. Despite the lead from Jamal, and his pal Freddie's vague description of a shapely woman in dark coveralls with long red nails and a tattoo on her wrist, Edward's investigative instincts were off.

On his advice, a warrant to search the CT labs had been secured. But Detective Grove and his crew had turned up nothing. The boxes of high-tech ammo Edward had found the night of the company's holiday party had been cleaned out. Not only was Blake Rivers's storage locker completely empty, but the shipping manifest he'd produced for Grove indicated that the order to ship the batch of "fishing weights" had come within the last twenty-four hours. He'd been behind every step of the way in his efforts to help his brothers and make good on the promise he'd made to his mother.

Bring his father's killer to justice and return John Kincaid's badge to her.

He hadn't been able to save his own family from André Butler's revenge—and he'd worked under-cover at Butler's side for months, had known him as well as he knew his own brothers. Why did he think he was cop enough to track down a stranger from his father's past and make things right for what was left of his family?

Maybe he'd better crawl back into his hole and let the professionals handle this.

"Must have been a rush order for the holidays." Detective Grove managed to keep his voice in a level tone when Edward's would have been laced with a good dose of sarcasm. "Tell me, is there a large market for fishing weights this time of year?"

Blake Rivers sat up straight in the interview chair beside his lawyer. "Different hemispheres of the world have different seasons, Detective Grove. The fish are biting in the South Pacific this time of year, and the industry there relies on our weights for their nets."

Unbelievable. The lying son of a bitch actually said that with a straight face. Edward scraped his palm over his jaw and shifted his weight off his right knee. What he'd found—what someone had nearly killed Holly for—wasn't any kind of fishing equipment. Unless some South Pacific islanders were taking up shooting fish for dinner. Grove better ask the right follow-up question, or this quest for answers would wind up just as fruitless as the empty storage locker.

Grove slowly leaned back in his chair. "You're telling me that a company as advanced at Caldwell Technologies is spending money manufacturing chunks of rock to keep fishing nets from floating away?"

"Nice one, Grove. Went right over his head." Edward's brothers were watching the questioning, too. Holden was shaking his head. "Do we really figure this Rivers is smart enough to be creating and shipping weapons and other technology through Caldwell Tech?"

"Think of what the alternative would mean." Atticus voiced what all of them were thinking. "If Rivers isn't bright enough to pull this off, then the only other person with access to the research labs, shipping schedules and inventories is Bill."

"No way could Bill Caldwell be behind anything that would hurt Dad." Sawyer voiced what they *wanted* to think. "He wouldn't hurt Mom."

"Unless he wanted Mom for himself," Holden suggested. Even Edward swung his gaze across the room and glared at that comment. But Holden wasn't backing down from his older brothers or his opinion. "He's been a widower for a long time. I never did like how fast he started putting the moves on Mom. Dad hasn't even been gone a year. Now Bill's at her house almost every night, or he's taking her out to some fancy place. I caught him kissing her one time—Edward, you saw that. Back in October at the house?"

He'd been clearing some of Cara and Melinda's things from the cabin that day, taking them to their mother's for a church rummage sale. It was the first time he could recall Bill Caldwell actually calling him "son." He'd used that term again the night of the holiday party. "I remember."

"And it wasn't a friendly peck-on-the-cheek kind of thing, either."

"She's a grown woman." Atticus attempted to insert a little reason into the emotions filling the room. "We can't decide who she likes or doesn't, just like we can't decide how long she's going to grieve or not."

"She's not done grieving," Sawyer insisted. "She still wears her wedding ring. She and Bill are just good friends."

Holden shrugged. "Does Bill know that?"

The voices on the other side of the glass were getting a little agitated as well.

Kevin Grove leaned forward. "You mean to tell me you're not bright enough to know what goes on in your own department?"

Blake Rivers shoved the paper work back across the table. "If the shipping order says fishing weights, then they were fishing weights. I don't know anything about these…disintegrator bullets you're talking about. Mr. Caldwell doesn't pay me to design weaponry like that."

"But he does pay you to design fishing weights?"

"No."

"Does he pay you to store boxes in your lab and not ask any questions? Because I've looked at your bank accounts, Rivers, and you've come into quite a bit of money recently." Grove inched in even closer. "Are you the smart guy who's running the show? Or the fall guy who doesn't know he's being used?"

Edward wouldn't have thought slow-talking Grove could push a suspect's buttons like that. But he had Rivers squeezing his fists on top of the table. Rivers's attorney whispered something into his client's ear. Then Pretty Boy took a deep breath and relaxed his hands. "My trust fund was recently activated," he answered on a calmer note. "That's where the influx of money into my accounts is coming from, not because of some illegal payoff or smuggling operation." Rivers turned his gaze toward the mirror. "Just because you have a renegade cop running around, sneaking into places he doesn't belong and making accusations against my character, doesn't mean you have a legitimate reason for holding me here. I know those Kincaids are out on some kind of vendetta, but I'm not the man they're after. And if they don't leave me alone, I may sue the department for harassment."

Renegade cop? Edward had called himself a lot worse.

"Harassment? Doesn't he know who—" When Holden jumped in to defend him, Edward put up a silencing hand. There was still something about Rivers that bugged him. Maybe it was just the fact that he'd been a jerk to Holly's sister, but he wanted to study him until he figured it out.

Unfortunately, they didn't have that kind of time.

"So, Detective Grove." Rivers stood and buttoned his suit jacket. "Are you going to charge me with something, or am I free to go?"

Grove stood on the opposite side of the table, his heavyweight wrestler's size making more than two of Rivers. Edward nearly smiled. He could have worked with a man like Kevin Grove. Deceptively smart. Tough. Hard to rile and harder to intimidate. "Of course, you're free to go, Mr. Rivers. I appreciate your willingness to answer my questions. Just don't leave town until we settle this issue of the missing fishing weights."

Rivers's cheeks reddened with a burst of temper and Pretty Boy didn't look so pretty anymore. "I have plans to travel to the Bahamas for the holidays."

"Change them."

Grove shuffled his papers back into his file and left. A minute later Blake Rivers stormed out, followed closely by his attorney and a warning that this was neither the time nor the place to blow off steam.

Feeling frustrated, weary—and like he just might want a drink—Edward inhaled a deep breath that seemed to take in all the air in the observation room. "This is like trying to put together a jigsaw puzzle without having any picture to go by. Caldwell Technologies, the disintegrator bullets, Holly's attack."

Atticus came up beside him at the window. "Dad's

journals, the fact that Brooke's mother, Irina Zorinsky, isn't the body we found buried beside her father."

Sawyer joined them. "The trail of dead bodies. Former operatives, all with the same tattoo or signature ring."

Holden wouldn't be left out. "Liza's eyewitness testimony places a woman, two of those dead operatives and an unknown man at the warehouse the night Dad was murdered."

"The pieces are all there, but we need some kind of reference so we know how to put it all together."

Edward felt all eyes looking at him.

"You're the leader of this family now," his mother had said. It was a responsibility he hadn't wanted. But he felt the weight of it squarely on his shoulders right now. His brothers had made headway in finding their father's killer, but someone needed to close this case. Someone needed to end this unjust hell and give his family peace.

Guess who?

The idea of an ice-cold beer to numb his throat and a few of his brain cells was sounding better and better with each passing moment.

"You guys will all be with Mom on Christmas Eve?" Edward asked.

"Yeah."

"Yes."

"Of course."

"Good." Edward turned and walked out the door.

He had a pretty good idea of what needed to be done to make this happen. But it would upset a family dynamic that had been with them for years, one that had given their mother inordinate comfort these past months since losing the love of her life. And it might just cost these good men that he loved their badges.

Edward wasn't sure he had one to lose.

BLAKE RIVERS'S SCOWLING FACE was not the one Holly had hoped to see when she stepped off the elevator of the Fourth Precinct's fourth floor.

"Oh, great. Just great," he whined when his blue eyes locked on to hers. "You just made my day, lady."

"Blake." Holly acknowledged him and stepped aside, eager to track down Edward and tell him about the DNA reports and that a supposedly dead woman was still very much alive.

But Blake was in a temper about something, and walking away from him apparently wasn't an option. Before she could get around him, his arm clotheslined across her chest and he backed her up against the wall beside the elevator. "You know, I'm trying to put my past behind me and lead a successful, normal life that my father would be proud of."

"Blake…" An older gentleman, most likely his attorney, tapped him on the shoulder. "I remind you, you're in a police station."

Blake shrugged him off. "I'm not touching her."

Indeed he wasn't now. But with his hand braced on the wall beside her head, the sleeve of his wool coat brushed against her hair. And the blockade of his arm and body meant she wasn't going anywhere unless she pushed him aside. In fact, from an outsider observer's point of view, it might have been a romantic stance between two lovers. If the words weren't so vile.

"It's always some uptight prick like you who brings up the drugs and the battery charges—which were all dismissed—"

"Pleaded out or reduced charges," she argued. "Just because you got community service instead of jail time doesn't mean you weren't guilty."

"—and ruins anything good I've got going on in my life."

"I'm sorry you're having a bad day, Blake." Holly didn't know why he was at the precinct office with a lawyer. She was pretty sure she didn't care, unless he'd done something to Jillian again. And she was certain she had neither the time nor the desire to stand here and bear the brunt of his temper. She flattened her hand at the center of his chest. "The day my sister came home with a black eye after spending the night with you is the day you lost any kind of consideration from me."

She pushed. He didn't budge.

His lawyer had his hands up in the air, as though

he didn't know how to handle his client's childish behavior, either. A frisson of panic quickened Holly's pulse and she tried to peek around Blake to get the attention of the woman working the sergeant's desk. But she was managing both the phone and a pair of visitors. Cubicle walls blocked her from the activity she could hear from the detectives' desks on the opposite side.

"Blake, we need to go," his attorney advised.

But Blake was on a tear and he needed to spew. "What kind of poison did you put into your sister's head? She used to be fun."

"You mean she used to cater to your every whim. She's healthy now. She stands on her own two feet. Jillian doesn't need your money or any of the drugs you supplied her anymore."

He pushed against her hand. "Sounds like slander to me, lady. I'm not that man anymore. I like Jillian. I bought tickets for us to take a vacation together."

"She won't go."

"You won't let her!"

The attorney tried one more time. "Blake, technically, you can't go, either."

"Shut up!"

All at once, Blake jerked back. Through a flurry of grunts and curses, she saw Edward behind him. Before Holly could do more than gasp, he had Blake shoved up against the wall, his neck pinned and his right arm trapped behind his back.

Edward put his mouth right up to Blake's ear. "You stay away from Holly and her sister. Understand?"

"Who the hell—"

"Understand?"

After a sharp twist pushed his face into the wall, Blake nodded.

Holly breathed a little easier after the unexpected rescue. "Edward. I'm so glad I found you."

But he wasn't listening to her. She wasn't quite sure *what* he was doing. Keeping Blake pinned with his body, Edward yanked up the ends of Blake's coat and suit sleeves.

"What the hell are you doing?" Blake demanded.

Edward answered by grabbing him by the collar and turning him around. "You're lucky you don't have a tattoo on your wrist."

"Why would I…?"

Edward's youngest brother, Holden, startled her when he gently pulled Holly away from the confrontation. He pushed the elevator's call button and the doors split open. "May I help?"

Edward nodded and pushed Blake toward his attorney. "Get him out of here."

Holden grinned. "I'd love to escort them down to the parking lot."

Blake straightened his clothes as he swung around. Holly instantly felt a grip on her arm and found herself standing behind the protective jut of

Edward's shoulder. "I am reporting you for police brutality," said the angry younger man.

Edward opened the front of his coat. "Do you see a badge on me?"

With Holden walking toward them, the lawyer pulled Blake inside the elevator. "At this point I'd advise you to shut your mouth, get over yourself and come with me."

Holden waved, a grown man delighted with the task given him. "See you later, bro. Doc."

After the doors closed, Holly grinned. "That lawyer actually said something I agree with."

"He should have intervened sooner." The vise holding her wrist softened. As Edward turned to face her, he ran his hands up her arms to her shoulders, hunching forward ever so slightly to look her in the eye and study her face. "Are you all right? What about your head?" His warm hands moved to the sides of her neck and tenderly cupped her jaw. "You didn't reinjure—"

"I'm okay." Holly reached up and wound her fingers around his wrists, trying to reach the concern she saw in his deep gray eyes and ease it from his expression. "I promise you, I'm okay. His arrogance annoys the heck out of me, but he didn't hurt me."

He eyed her a moment longer, not quite believing her. "Good." Then he leaned in and pressed a quick, hard kiss to her lips and pulled away before she could properly return the favor. "Now what are you doing here? I thought I told you to stay at home and rest."

Holly pulled his hands from her face and laced their fingers together between them. "You said if I went somewhere that the patrolman had to come with me. He drove me to the lab and now he's waiting downstairs with some friends of his."

He tugged on her hands to pull her aside as the elevator doors opened and a trio of uniformed officers stepped out. "Do you have any idea how hard it is for me to do my job when I'm worried about you?"

Holly smiled at the hidden message she heard. He wouldn't be so worried if he didn't care about her. Maybe more than he even knew. But she'd called and deduced and tracked him here because she needed to talk business right now. Forcing him to admit that this was a real relationship growing between them would have to wait.

Letting go of his hands reluctantly, she reached into her purse and pulled out the copies she'd made of the lab reports. "I brought these to show Kevin Grove, but I want you to see them first."

"What are they?"

"Proof that Irina Zorinsky Hansford is still alive and that I think I know how to bring her out of hiding."

"No." His gray eyes bored into hers. "I will not agree to anything that puts you in more danger."

Holly pulled away entirely and crossed her arms in a defiant stance. *She* was the one still wearing the official credentials here. "I wasn't asking for permission. You can either work with me or you can work against me. Now I have a feeling that we'd do much better as a team, but I'll let that be your call." She wanted to touch him, throttle him, beg him to understand that the answers to an eight-month long investigation were within their grasp. "We can crack this case, Edward. We can put your father's killer away."

His mouth thinned into a grim line. "Don't do something crazy, Holly. I may not be able to protect you. I have a lead myself I want to pursue—"

"On your own? Can I come with you?"

"No. Absolutely not." He raked his fingers through his hair, leaving a sexy disarray that her fingers itched to smooth back into place. "It's personal. I need to do this on my own so it doesn't come back to bite any of my brothers in the butt. Or you."

"If it's something that can get you into trouble, you should let me see what I—"

"No! I want you to go home, lock yourself in your apartment and be safe. Let me take care of this."

Holly's lips parted in shock at the vehemence of his argument. How damaged did a man have to be that he could only allow himself to see the world in one isolating, dangerous, forget-about-anyone-else's-wishes-or-feelings kind of way?

"Edward, you can't control who gets hurt and who doesn't." She gestured toward the sounds of the cops doing their work behind those cubicle walls. "Yes, this is dangerous work. And sometimes innocent people get hurt. But I'm trained to do my job. I'm trained to be smart and watch my back and get the bad guys, all at the same time. I'm going to do my job. With or without your help."

"Taking on Z Group is suicide."

"That's what they used to say about taking on André Butler. And you defeated him."

"No, Stick. I lost. I lost everything." He smacked his hand against the elevator door and Holly jumped at the sudden outburst of his frustration and emotion. "Look at me. I'm not the man who took on Butler. I'm beat-up, I'm out of practice and my head's not in the game the way it used to be. I thought you were dead when I saw you in that autopsy drawer with all that blood. When I saw Blake Rivers accosting you just now, I nearly lost it."

"He wasn't hurting me."

"I know. And I still…overreacted." Edward's eyes were looking everywhere but at her. He was searching for words, searching for reason. "I can't…" He swallowed hard, then determinedly looked her in the eye. "I can't care about you if you're going to intentionally put yourself in danger."

"If we're a team, it won't be so dangerous. I

watch your back. You watch mine. There's no one I trust more than you to keep me safe."

"That'd be your mistake."

"Your wife and daughter didn't die because of any mistake *you* made."

"I put them in harm's way. I made them targets. And now I've gotten you so involved in my father's murder that I've made you a target."

"Edward, please." She curled her fingers into the front of his sweater, trying to reach the man inside. "It was a tragedy, yes, and you paid a huge price. But think of all the lives you saved by getting rid of Butler. Think of the lives we can save by exposing Irina Zorinsky and Z Group. It's not just about us," she pleaded with the man she couldn't help loving, despite his harsh words. "Help me."

"I'm sorry." He pulled her fingers off him and re-treated. "I just can't do this. I can't lose you, too." The elevator doors opened and he walked inside. When he reached the back wall, he turned around and offered her one last bleak pronouncement. "You're on your own. Good luck."

The doors closed.

They closed around her heart, too.

"What about Grandpa, Daddy? You promised."

Edward sat in the living room of his stone cabin, isolated in the snowy countryside on the outskirts of Kansas City's metropolitan area. Late-night television provided the only light in the entire house, but he wasn't really watching. He slouched back against the black leather sofa, his booted feet propped up on the coffee table beside two cartons holding eleven bottles of ice-cold imported beer.

He twirled the twelfth bottle unopened in his right hand, savoring the chill of the icy condensation dripping over his fingers, barely able to hear his daughter's voice.

A box that he'd pulled down from a closet shelf sat open on the coffee table. He'd tried to give some of the items away—but his mother and youngest brother had insisted he keep the contents that had once held meaning for him. Inside the box were painful reminders of his past. His badge. His gun. A wedding picture with Cara. A child's rag doll ornament with button eyes that had been glued on crookedly. The ornament had been Melinda's gift to him that last morning, just before he drove away to pick up her new bike. She'd given them a handmade present that she'd made at her school because she was too excited to wait until Christmas.

Tonight he'd gotten the cockeyed notion in his head that if he could look at those things that had once meant so much to him and not fall apart, then maybe he stood half a chance at making something happen with Holly. Maybe he could be a cop. Maybe he could feel like a real human being again.

Walking away from Holly this afternoon had been a selfish thing to do. The coward's way out of getting hurt.

And tonight he hurt, anyway.

"Be brave, Daddy."

"I'm trying, baby," he whispered into the darkness. Trying and failing.

He'd already destroyed one family connection tonight. Before stopping to buy the beer, he'd paid a visit to William Caldwell. He'd asked the man flat-out how much he knew about Z Group's current activities, how much he might still be an active part of them and if he knew that Irina Zorinsky Hansford was still alive.

Bill had gone pale. Poured himself a brandy before saying a word.

Yeah, there was something to tell. Either he'd just seen a ghost, or he'd been caught in the biggest lie of their lives.

"Alive? Irina is alive?" Edward had seen better acting jobs from doped-up street punks trying to talk their way out of a possession charge.

All these months since his father's murder—all these years that they'd spent together on camping and fishing trips, holiday get-togethers, graduations and other special events—Bill Caldwell had been lying.

He knew about Irina. Knew about Z Group.

Why give him clearance to search the labs at

Caldwell Technologies? Not to point the finger at Blake Rivers, but to ease his own conscience.

Edward half hoped that Bill would say something about being blackmailed, about having no choice but to do an evil woman's bidding—that he was a victim like the rest of them. Instead, he claimed to know nothing about his father's murder or Holly's attack or any other thing that Irina Zorinsky had been responsible for.

Oh, he told him plenty about the old days, when Z Group had been a government-sanctioned organization monitoring the flow of weapons and technology throughout eastern Europe before the fall of Communist regimes. He talked about the beautiful Irina—the double agent who had planned to hand over their names to their enemies—how they'd met secretly and taken a vote to eliminate her. He told him how Irina's besotted husband, Leo Hansford, had volunteered for the mission to kill them both in a car accident.

"But Atticus's fiancée, Brooke Hansford—Leo and Irina's daughter—went to Sarajevo to move her parents' remains back to the States. We told you that the DNA tests proved that the body buried in Irina's grave wasn't Irina. Didn't you suspect anything then? Or are you the reason she's still alive today?"

"She can't be alive." It had taken another brandy for Bill to finally start sounding like the self-made billionaire he was. He'd accused Edward of lying, of manufacturing stories to trip him up like some common criminal. He was throwing out cruel guesses, trying to stir up a suspect because KCPD had been working eight months on this and still couldn't make a case. *"Crawl back into your hole, Edward, and stop trying to be a hero. How could you accuse me of being a part of your father's murder? I loved John like a brother. I love you and your brothers as if you were my own sons. I love your mother. Why would I agree to allow the people I love to be hurt?"*

Feeling the lies like whip marks over his soul, Edward had stood up to make his exit. *"Think about this, Bill. If you know about Irina and you don't do anything to stop her, then you might lose more of the people you love. Their lives would be on your head.*

"And trust me, you don't want to be in that place."

When he walked away, it had almost been like losing his father all over again. He'd made the accusations his brothers hadn't been able to make. He'd severed a bond that had been a part of his life from the day he was born. And someone else he loved had just been lost to him forever.

Now he was sitting alone, with late-night television shows droning on like crickets in the darkness, debating whether or not eight months of sobriety was worth the pain of caring about things.

It had to be better not to care about Holly, right?

Better not to want her with every cell in his body.

Better not to see her as the first light of something good to come into his life since losing Cara and Melinda?

He squeezed the bottle's cap within his fist and considered turning it.

He was saving them both from a big world of hurt, right?

"…Holly Masterson, medical examiner with the KCPD crime lab. Dr. Masterson…"

"What the…?" The words from his TV set suddenly became important.

Switching out the beer for the remote, Edward turned up the volume. The nosy blond reporter who'd tried to stop him at the lab, Hayley Resnick, was recapping a news report, covering the highlights of a KCPD news conference held earlier in the evening. The picture switched from Ms. Resnick to taped footage of the news conference.

Edward's heavy boots thumped to the floor as he sat forward. Unbelievable. Did that woman have a death wish?

Flanked by Mitch Taylor and Detective Kevin Grove, Holly stood at the press room podium, waiting to address the reporter's question. "Dr. Masterson. Is it true that your lab has found conclusive results confirming that Cold War operative Irina Zorinsky Hansford is still alive?"

"Yes. Her DNA turned up at a recent crime scene."

"Can you elaborate?"

Holly tucked her short hair behind her ears. "I'm afraid I can't comment as it's part of an ongoing investigation. But I assure you, the results are conclusive. She is alive."

Dissatisfied with that answer, Ms. Resnick turned her microphone toward the officer in charge. "Major Taylor, I see you're standing in for the commissioner while she's away on vacation. Can you tell our viewers—does Ms. Zorinsky pose a significant threat to the Kansas City community? Is this something Homeland Security will look into?"

KCPD could place a woman matching Irina's general description at two different locations—one of which was Holly's attack—and they thought it was a smart idea to splash Holly's face all over the television?

Edward rose to his feet. Was *this* Holly's idea? Flush Irina Zorinsky out of hiding? And what was Taylor thinking? That Holly's pretty face and brainy deductions made the perfect bait?

Edward snatched his cell phone off its charger, intending to punch in Major Taylor's number and warn him of the danger Holly could be in. But when he turned it on, three voice mail messages popped up, all from Holly. She was probably just checking up on him, being strong and sensible and braver about their growing feelings than he'd been. But if any one of them included the word *help* or *danger*, then he'd probably just tumble right over the edge into the bottle that was now leaving a ring of moisture on his coffee table.

Edward turned away from the temptation and played the first message. Holly was looking for him. Why didn't he answer his phone? The second message was similar, leaving her sister Jillian's cell phone number as well as her work phone in case he wanted to contact her. The third—

The knock at his front door was as startling as any cry for help. Ages ago, he would have sensed the unwelcome guest and identified him already. Tonight, he hadn't even heard a car drive up. Every muscle inside him tensed before he closed his phone and set it on the table. The hour was late, the cabin dark, the location remote. This couldn't be any accidental tourist stopping by.

The box containing his past life was right there beside his hand. With defensive instincts and old cautions surfacing inside him, it felt only natural to reach for the gun and pull it from its holster. It hadn't been cleaned in two years, but then it hadn't been used, either.

He was unboxing a clip of bullets when his visitor knocked again. Louder this time. "Edward? Are you awake?"

"Holly?" His ankle and knee protested the sudden

spin toward the door. But other pangs moved him even faster. "Holly?"

He tucked his gun in the back of his jeans and swung the door open to find her standing on *his* screened-in porch. Bundled up and dotted with snow on his porch. "I know it's late, but—"

"Get in here." He pulled her inside, taking note of the black-and-white unit making a U-turn in his drive and pulling away. He scanned the woods and gravel road beyond, searching for any sign of being tailed, before closing the door and pushing her against the thick stones and beams of the wall. "Where's your escort going?"

"He's been with me all day and night. I told him once I got inside with you he could go home to his own family."

"Call him back."

He was still shielding her with his body from a threat he knew was out there, somewhere, when her gloved hand came up to brush against the stubble of his jaw. "You didn't return any of my calls. I was worried. I didn't want to leave it like it was between us this afternoon. I think we need to talk."

Wants and needs lurched inside him in response to her determined tenderness. But something harder, self-preserving, made him reach up and pull her hand away. "Do you have any idea how much I *don't* want to talk?"

Her gaze moved beyond him to the coffee table. "But you're willing to get drunk?"

"I saw your news conference. Taylor shouldn't have put you up to that."

"I volunteered. This case is about to break wide open. I'm about to find the answers I've been searching eight months for."

"No. No way, Stick." He raked his fingers through his hair and turned away, crossing to the table and placing the loose bottle back in the carton with its golden, frosty mates. "This is *my* war to fight against Z Group. Not yours. I want you off my father's murder investigation. I'm prepared to deal with the mess that's coming down the road. But I don't want you anywhere near it."

Her footsteps followed him into the kitchen. "You're armed and sitting in the dark with twelve beers? That's what you call prepared? I was right to be worried."

"Here." He pulled his phone from his pocket and held it out to her. "Call your backup guy back, and have him drive you home. Or better yet, to a safe house."

Bright lights flooded the kitchen, forcing him to close his eyes. "Stick." Any argument died when he felt her press her face against his chest. Cells in his body leaped to life. She turned her nose to the juncture of his neck and shoulder and his pulse raced. She framed his face and tilted her head back.

His arms went round her and he lowered his mouth, helplessly drawn to her kiss. But the surge of passion came to a cruelly abrupt halt when she sniffed. And then she was prying open his eyelids. "What are you doing?"

"You haven't had anything to drink yet?" Her hazel eyes studied his, looking for answers that went beyond the physical. Looking hopeful.

He squeezed her shoulders and pushed her away. "No."

"Then call your sponsor and go to a meeting before you do. Please."

This woman was unbelievable. She'd just revealed her knowledge of a dangerous killer on a public newscast and she was worried about *him*? He released her entirely. "Look, you do not need to deal with the likes of me. You already have one addict in your family—that's more than any one person should have to take care of."

"Jillian's a recovering addict," she corrected. "And you're the one who reminded me that it isn't my job to 'take care' of her. She has to take care of herself. I just have to love her."

Her green-gold eyes reached all the way into his heart, stunning him like an electric shock, bringing something back to life inside him.

No. He couldn't hear those words. Couldn't dare feel them or believe what they implied.

He gripped the edge of the counter behind him.

Gripped it with both hands. "Let me solve Dad's murder on my own, Stick. Leave me alone and let me work. You don't have to worry about me."

"I've watched Jillian heal, Edward. You can, too. I *need* you to heal."

"So I can keep you safe? You know how well I protected my own family."

"Please." She had the brass to reach right into his pocket and pull out the keys to his Jeep. "Let me take you to the meeting, Edward. And then…we'll come back here." Her hands might be bold, but vulnerability softened her eyes and sentenced him to the truth. His efforts to free himself from his feelings for Holly Masterson had come too late. "You may want to get rid of me, but I have no intention of leaving you."

Chapter Ten

"Satisfied?"

He watched her slide the last stack of bills back into the envelope he'd given her, and then tuck it into her trinket box along with the other spoils from her work here in the United States. She'd counted out the entire $100,000, not trusting him for one minute, even after all this time together.

She reached up to trace his mouth with one red-tipped finger. "Now that's a loaded question, isn't it, dear? You know my appetites are insatiable."

He kissed the fingertip because she expected him to. But his mind was already racing ahead to the plans he'd made following his visit from Edward Kincaid earlier in the evening.

Edward—who suspected everything but couldn't prove it.

If he was anything like his father—and he was—then it was only a matter of time before Edward found that proof.

He'd already buried his best friend because of this woman.

William Caldwell wasn't going to stay around long enough to see his best friend's oldest son buried alongside him. The game was finally up. But Bill had one last play to make.

After she zipped the trinket box into her carry-on bag, Bill tossed a pair of airline tickets onto the bed beside her. It had to be two tickets because even with all her conniving intellect and complete lack of remorse for the vicious retributions she'd handed out over the years, Irina Zorinsky had one fatal flaw.

She hated to be alone.

It was her *insatiable* need for male companionship that had doomed him to this deadly alliance in the first place. If he hadn't been sleeping with her thirty years ago, she never would have discovered that *he* was the one who'd been selling American technology and the names of Z Group operatives to their enemies. She never would have discovered how lucrative playing both sides of the spy game could be and demanded to be cut in on a piece of the profits. She never would have hatched that ludicrous plan to take the blame and "die" in his place, thereby setting up a secret partnership that allowed him to be the straight, upstanding American entrepreneur while she sold his company's technology abroad without fear of being caught. After all, how could Interpol or the CIA or anyone else track a dead woman?

Over the years she'd proved to be a perfect partner. In exchange for a little sex and a lot of money, she took care of any problems that came up. She knew how to entice reliable help to work for them and how to dispose of unreliable ones.

And any time she began to think that *he* was becoming an unreliable partner, she only had to remind him that she knew as much about his illegal activities as he did about hers. Killing her for real had never been an option because she'd hidden clues about him on two different continents. If something ever happened to her, he didn't doubt that some mysterious package would show up on Interpol's doorstep, naming names and pointing the finger straight at him.

But he'd never thought about killing himself before.

The ruse had worked so well for her, why not for him? It was his turn to disappear, to leave this life behind. To take his money and be rid of her and finally find some peace.

But first, he had to get her on that plane.

"You're awfully quiet." She picked up the tickets and read the first-class schedule for a flight to Rio de Janeiro. She'd like the heat there. "It makes me nervous when you spend so much time thinking, dear. Makes me wonder if you're up to something."

Realizing that his cover was slipping, he plucked the tickets from her fingers and pulled her into his arms. Her curves settled against him in that familiar decadent fit, and he reminded himself that the sex between them would have to end. He kissed her lips. "I'm just worried you'll change your mind about going. Life as Senhor and Senhora Smith is going to be a lot less exciting than what we've been used to."

And then he reached for the zipper of her dress. She reached for *his* zipper, making it hard to focus on his plan. "You're not thinking that a hundred grand is enough for us to live on, are you?"

"I told you, it's just spending cash for the trip. I'll take care of setting up our new home in Brazil, I promise. But I can't just write a check for seventy-five million dollars without making my accountants suspicious. Don't worry. I've set up a charitable trust that will pay us on a regular basis."

"Good." She pushed him back on the bed beside her luggage and climbed on top of him. "Because just 'spending cash' will never be enough for me."

It was sometime later, after she'd had her way with him and he was drifting off to sleep that Bill remembered the most dangerous part of his plan. It wasn't staging a fatal car accident while she waited for him at the airport.

It was getting out of the country with a woman he could really love.

Irina wasn't the only one who hated to be alone.

THOUGH EDWARD'S RUSTIC CABIN was devoid of any Christmas decorations whatsoever, Holly felt cozy and warm and curiously at home as she explored the kitchen and main rooms.

Maybe it was because the place felt so much like the man who owned it. The masculine style of the exposed wood beams and leather furniture reminded her of Edward's dark hair and earthy scent. The quiet, isolated location and unyielding strength of the rock walls fit, too.

And inside the spare, forbidding exterior, she'd found glimpses of tenderness and sentimentality and love.

Like the sweet, handmade doll she'd put in a place of honor on the mantel above the fireplace where she'd lit a small, warming fire. Obviously made by a child's hand, the rag doll angel was crafted of ticking and yarn and glue. The crooked design of its eyes and mouth made her think of a fresh-faced smile, and she wondered if it reminded him of his daughter. Or was the dusty ornament a treasured memento from his past life?

Holly had already dumped the beer down the sink and tossed the bottles into the trash. Whether he believed it or not, he'd made her feel safe here. She wanted him to feel safe, too.

After hanging up their coats, Edward had checked the locks on every door and window and headed straight for the shower. He hadn't said more than five words on the drive back from the midnight AA meeting. But it wasn't the moody, brooding quiet of a man dealing with internal demons. It had been a silence of inevitability, an acceptance that something had changed irrevocably between them. She'd broken down walls tonight by practically confessing the love that was growing in her heart. He was dealing with that. Maybe deciding what his own feelings were, maybe deciding he wasn't ready to deal with feelings yet.

She'd give him the time and the space to let him deal.

But she wasn't walking away from him. He couldn't scare her off with his grouchy tempers or his dire words about somehow failing her. Edward Kincaid didn't need someone to love him in order to heal and believe in himself again.

He needed to *give* love to someone else. He needed to learn that he *could* love again.

And she was here to volunteer for the job.

"Cold?"

Holly startled at the deep, gravelly voice behind her. But it was a welcome sound. She held her palms out toward the fire, warming away the hint of goose bumps that lingered on her skin. "A little. I haven't been around a real fireplace in years. I'd forgotten how wintry and festive it makes me…" *Oh, man.* "…feel."

She caught a delicious whiff of spicy shower gel and steamy male skin a heartbeat before Edward's broad bare shoulders came into view. He walked past her to the woodbin next to the hearth, wearing nothing but a pair of dark blue jeans, unsnapped at the waist and riding low around his hips. With shameless fascination, Holly watched the flexes and swells of muscle along his shoulders, arms and tapering back as he pulled aside the fire screen and added a couple of large logs to the flames. "That should keep things burning all night."

Holly felt that double entendre all the way down to her toes, though he'd been talking temperature, not lusty surges through the blood. She licked her lips, feeling a sudden thirst. Beat-up, as he'd described himself, looked mighty good on him. "Aren't *you* cold?"

He shrugged, shifting the muscles and her hormones all over again. "I'm used to it." He proceeded to stir the fire and secure the screen. He combed his fingers through his still-damp hair and then he made yet another trip around the cabin, rechecking the double lock on the front door and making sure the windows and shutters were all locked up tight.

Though she stayed by the fire's warmth, Holly's curiosity seemed to have a mind of its own, taking in several quick observations. Edward worked out—not to any sculpted pretty-boy extreme, but he was healthy and fit and more nicely put together than she'd expected for a man who'd most likely been bedridden or confined to a wheelchair for months. The scars that lined his jaw and neck peppered down across his torso as well, creating tiny voids in the coffee-dark curls that sprinkled across his chest and tapered down to disappear behind the open snap of his jeans. His limp was still there, but barely discernible as he moved with the efficiency of a trained guard dog, making her feel, ridiculously, more secure than she'd felt standing at precinct headquarters, surrounded by cops.

When he came back to her side, one final observation revealed a round, puckered scar on his chest, up near his right shoulder, that she recognized from too many autopsies. Scientific curiosity became a woman's concern and she lifted her fingers to gently trace the badge of honor on his skin. "When were you shot?"

His skin pulsed beneath her touch and she quickly drew her hand away, singed by a heat far more seductive than the warmth of the fire. "André Butler shot me…that morning." His words were low and precise, yet laced with an emotion she couldn't quite name. "He incapacitated my arm, nicked a lung. That's why I had to use my truck to run him down. I didn't have any other weapon I could use when he fired on me again. Smacking into a row of cars and a tree did the rest of the damage."

"Oh, my God. Edward." Holly automatically reached for him again, feeling the pain of all that was left unsaid in his clinical report.

But the instant her hand touched his shoulder, he

pulled away, as though a shock had passed between them. He splayed his hands at the flat of his stomach, modestly covering himself as he faced her. He'd revealed too much, and it had nothing to do with bare skin. "Sorry. I don't own a robe. I usually just go straight from the shower to… Ah, whatever. I'll go put a shirt on."

"No, don't." She grabbed hold of his arm to stop him from leaving. His skin seared her, hot from the heat of the fire, hotter still from the man within. But this time, Holly didn't pull away. "I mean, don't change your routine on my account."

"Holly…" He reached over to free himself from her restraining touch. But his hand slid over hers and remained in place instead. His gravelly voice dropped in pitch, creating the most seductive of whispers. "Asking for your help on Dad's murder has already turned my life upside down. I don't think adjusting my wardrobe is a big deal at this point."

Holly frowned. "Is that a joke, Lieutenant?"

"It's a statement of fact." With the hint of a smile curving his lips, Edward released her and stalked across the room to a hall closet. "I set up my weight-training equipment in the spare room, so there's no bed. You'll have to make do with some blankets and a pillow on the couch."

"The couch will be fine." Feeling an inexplicable chill despite standing so close to the fire, Holly hugged her arms around her waist. "It was good enough for you at my place. It will be good enough for me here."

He tossed a pillow at one end of the long, wide sofa and spread a cotton blanket over the leather upholstery. "Of course, after broadcasting to a killer that you know she's still alive and that you have the means to link her to several murders, I'd rather you lock yourself in a safe house." He pushed a thick wool blanket into her arms, indicating her bed was ready. "But since you won't listen to that kind of common sense, I guess my couch will have to do."

How could she get it through his thick skull that *this* was where she wanted to be? That she trusted him above anyone else to protect her from the dangers of the world outside? He cared about her as a man, not just a cop doing his job. Didn't he see that that's what set him apart from any other bodyguard KCPD could assign to her? "Edward, I—"

"Good night, Stick." He smoothed her bangs off her forehead and tucked them behind her ear. Holly felt the soft caress deep inside her heart. And when he leaned in, she was already bracing her hand against his chest, rising up onto her toes for his kiss.

His mouth opened over hers, tender and warm, gently demanding as he stroked his tongue across the seam of her lips and slipped inside. Hugging the folded blanket between them, Holly drifted forward, drawn to his tenderness, seeking his heat.

She touched the tip of her tongue to his, and he moaned. Holly smiled against his mouth.

This man knew how to love. He knew how to care. He just had to believe that he could—

He pulled away with a determined breath, abruptly ending the kiss. "Good night."

She watched him walk into his bedroom and close the door. Disappointment for them both left her shivering in her boots. When she was alone, she whispered, "Good night."

Holly unzipped her boots and stripped down to her camisole and jeans before sliding under the blanket. The wool was scratchy against her bare skin but surprisingly toasty. She had the crackling sounds of the fire, its flickering light and its pervasive warmth to soothe her to sleep.

Yet, according to the time on Jillian's cell phone, more than a half hour passed and she was still sitting up, curled into a ball beneath the blanket at the corner of the couch and feeling unsettled inside. She'd like to blame the unfamiliar quiet of the snowy rural night, but she knew it was the unfamiliar longing inside her that was keeping her awake.

She was considering searching Edward's kitchen cabinets for tea to brew when she heard the cursing coming from his room. She heard something like a stomp and froze. Had he knocked something over? Was he having a nightmare? Should she go to him and try to wake him?

Holly jerked when the bedroom door swung open.

Her breath came in deep, stuttering gasps as Edward stopped in the archway leading to the other rooms. The oranges and golds of the fire glimmered off his chest—his breathing was deep and uneven as well. His face was wreathed in shadows but she could feel the intensity of his gaze focused solely on her.

"I can't fall asleep, woman." Like a leviathan emerging from the shadowy deep, Edward stalked across the room, heading straight toward her. A surge of base female awareness heated Holly's blood and opened her pores. But an equally instinctive reaction—fight or flight—had her twisting to uncurl her legs from beneath her and get to her feet before he came close. But it was too late. "Scoot over."

"Edward?"

He came down on the couch beside her, his arms wrapping around both her and the blanket as he pulled her onto his lap.

Was this safe? Was she safe? She flattened her palms against his chest and pushed.

But he easily overpowered her and fell back onto the cushions, stretching her out across the top of him. With her arms trapped between them, she couldn't catch herself. Her breasts pillowed and beaded against the impact with his harder muscles. Her legs tangled and fell on either side of his, opening herself to the press of a rock-hard thigh. As she helplessly rode the rise and fall of his chest, her blood turned to liquid heat and pooled at the tips of her breasts and deeper within.

He pulled the blanket loose and spread it across her back, capturing the nape of her neck and curve of her bottom in his hands as he rolled onto his side, spilling her between the back of the couch and the heat of his body. "This is what you want, isn't it?" he growled against her ear. "Because it's what I want. I can't sleep a lick, knowing you're out here by yourself, closer to the doors, the windows, the danger."

"Sleep? You're talking sleep?" Holly wedged her arms between them and tried to give her body some room to recover from the leaping, needy impulses that made her want to snuggle even closer.

"Shh." He hushed her with his voice and stroked his fingers through the hair at her temple, trying to soothe her. "For now, Stick. I can't relax, knowing that falling asleep would leave you unguarded." He threw one heavy leg over hers, emphasizing his point. "But if I can hold you, touch you, keep you close—then some part of me will know you're safe. Is that okay?" He tipped her chin, asking her to read the sincerity in his eyes. "I need that to be okay."

What she read in his face instantly calmed her. The cells in her body were still simmering with an untapped awareness of every texture, every temptation of his body molded to hers. But she felt something deeper, more profound, that allowed her to take a deep, steadying breath. "You want to hold me?"

He nodded, his callused fingers gently moving against her face again. "If I don't get any sleep, I won't be any good to you."

Holly reached up and matched the subtle caresses across his cheek and jaw. She smiled, gently soothing the unsettled beast inside him. "Holding me would be very okay."

With a deep sigh, she felt him relax. He rolled onto his back, keeping his arms around her as she snuggled against his side and used the jut of his shoulder for her pillow.

They lay in comfortable silence for a few minutes longer before Edward spoke. She heard his voice as a rumble in his chest beneath her ear. "I see you already made yourself at home. I guess I like that there."

She turned her head to see him looking at the rag doll ornament on the mantel. "Did your daughter make that for you?

"Yeah."

"Tell me about her."

She felt a tension come into his body as he began to talk. "Melinda was a special little girl, blond and beautiful like her mother." Holly didn't move as he began to stroke his hand up and down her back. "We found out while Cara was pregnant that she was going to be a Down's syndrome baby and that we wouldn't know what kind of mental or physical handicaps she might have until she was born."

Holly's arm went around his waist and she hugged him with her whole body. "I imagine you were given options about her birth."

"Terminating the pregnancy or giving up the child was never an option for us. If any woman was ever meant to be a mother, it was Cara Fitzpatrick. I wasn't sure a tough guy like me was up to the task, but from the moment I held Melinda in my arms, I became a daddy."

His hand stopped at her waist and tears burned in Holly's eyes. She blinked them away and pressed a kiss to his pectoral, urging him to continue. Edward's hand began to stroke her again, this time sliding beneath her camisole to maintain skin-to-skin contact, as if he needed that human touch in order to speak. Each brush of his callused fingertips was like the kiss of a cat's tongue, stoking the heat simmering inside her. "Melinda was the embodiment of love. Had her grandpa wrapped around her finger, gave my mom a little girl to play with that she'd never had before. She accepted everything and everyone. The terrible hours and dangers of my job, the fact she was behind other kids her age in school. Cara was wonderful with her. She kept trying to turn her into a little lady, but I made her a tomboy. We practiced for Special Olympics events together—the preliminary events, she wasn't quite old enough or coordinated enough to compete at the regional meets. She played a mean kickball and loved her art classes. She was always a happy, intuitive little girl."

"Intuitive? How do you mean?"

He tunneled his fingers into Holly's hair and kissed her forehead. That's when she realized hers weren't the only eyes that had filled with tears. "Melinda could read my moods. She knew when something at work was weighing on my mind. She knew when something bad had happened and I needed to snap out of it and have some fun. Sometimes…" His arms tightened almost painfully around her before relaxing. "I still hear her voice in my head. Encouraging me when I can't see the daylight. Telling me the right thing to do. Lecturing me when I'm being stupid."

A laugh vibrated through Edward's body, and Holly smiled. "You loved her with all your heart, didn't you."

He nodded. "I've always had a thing for strong women. You know, the reason I'm not too big on the season is…" His arms tightened again. When they didn't relax, Holly didn't complain. "Her last words to me…"

His ragged, pain-filled breath tore at Holly's heart. She wriggled her arms free and propped herself up on one elbow, crying herself as she caressed the lines of sorrow from beside his taut mouth. "What did Melinda say?"

His eyes crinkled and the tears spilled over. "She was lying there in the snow beside Cara's body, her own precious life seeping away, and she said... 'Merry Christmas, Daddy.' She was still happy, still trying to make me feel better, and she said, 'Merry Christmas.'"

She kissed a tear from the corner of his mouth, kissed another from his cheek and wept along with him.

"Sounds like she was saying, 'I love you'."

"Yeah." Edward's gaze focused, tearing himself from the past and looking up into her eyes. He was with her now. With her in the warm, soothing dark on this couch. Putting the past to rest. Seeing *her*. Healing. "Yeah. She was saying, 'I love you.'"

The intensity of the emotions he'd shared blended with the heat stirring between them and transformed into something else entirely. Healing took on a new form as he slipped both hands beneath her camisole and skimmed it off over her head. With little to cover, Holly rarely wore a bra and Edward's hungry gaze seemed to appreciate that fact.

Aligning her squarely over his body, he pulled one breast into his mouth, the straining tip eagerly budding as he swirled his tongue around the sensitive nipple. Spikes of red-hot desire arrowed through her, landing straight in her womb and making her hips twist against his, seeking release.

Holly cradled his head between her hands, guiding his wicked tongue to the other breast. She pressed kisses to his hair and gasped as he pulled on her, igniting a liquid fire in her veins. "Edward..." His hips bucked beneath her and Holly's thighs spread open. "Ed..."

He abandoned her breasts to capture her mouth and take her in a thorough, drugging kiss that reached into her heart and granted him whatever he wanted, whatever he needed from her.

The hands that had roamed across her back slid lower, dipping into the waistband of her jeans. Holly ran her hands over his chest, curling hairs prickling her palms and exciting her skin. As one hand slipped deeper beneath the denim to squeeze her bottom, the other came around to work the snap and zipper of her jeans.

"I need you, Stick." He nipped at her chin. Tongued the spot and nipped her again. "I need you."

"Yes." The bulge inside his jeans pushed against her hip and she instinctively moved to cradle him. "Yes."

His breath was hot and moist and erratic as he inched his way toward her breasts again. "Tell me to back off now, or this is gonna happen."

Holly pulled his mouth back to hers and kissed

him hard, squeezing him through their jeans. "Trust me, sweetheart, my answer is yes."

With a sweep of motion and a creak of leather and a dozen more kisses, Holly was naked, pinned beneath Edward's strong, male body. He'd paused long enough to cover himself, but now he was stretching her arms above her head, nudging her thighs apart with his knee, and she was loving it. Loving him.

He entered her slowly and Holly arched at the almost instantaneous heat that burst into flame at the spot where their bodies joined, groaning with delight as she adjusted to take more of him. "Are you all right?" He quickly withdrew, grunting at the effort it took to hold himself back. "I'm so out of practice. If I hurt you—"

"Damn it, Edward." She pulled her hands free and forced him to look her in the eye. "You did not hurt me. You *will* not hurt me. Not with this or anything else. I'm one of those strong women you talked about. The ones you can't resist? I want you in me. Now."

He smiled.

"That I can do."

He took her in one long stroke and Holly convulsed around him. By the time he'd pumped his release inside her, she was crying out his name, shouting out her pleasure and welcoming him straight into her heart.

SOMETIME DURING THE NIGHT, Edward roused himself from the clinging delight of Holly's naked body. His first intention had been to retrieve the blanket that had fallen to the floor so he could cover her. But now he found the blanket hanging from his hand while he watched her sleep.

As the glow from the firelight warmed her creamy skin, he checked her from head to toe, looking for bruises or any other kind of injury or discomfort he might have caused her. He touched a dark spot here. No, just a shadow. He brushed a pink abrasion on the swell of her breast, wishing he'd taken the time to shave before he'd left the mark of passion on her.

He dipped his nose into the sugary vanilla warmth of her hair, breathing in her scent as he draped the blanket around her. He didn't have any problem keeping her warm on a winter's night with the shelter of his body, but he thought he should do something a little more tender, show her a little more finesse, than that bull-in-a-china-shop rut she'd shared with him earlier.

Despite her claim that she was a strong woman— and in countless ways, she was—Holly was also a woman who had stitches in her head and a hugely compassionate heart. She'd cried at the tragic beauty of Melinda's short life, had shared his sorrow and listened and kissed away his own tears.

And then, when the emotions became too much—

while the barriers were down and he could no longer filter his reactions through the mores of polite society, she'd given him her body. She'd offered herself like a balm to his ravaged soul, and he'd taken everything she was willing to give. Edward had buried himself so deep inside her that he lost himself. He hadn't felt the pain then, hadn't felt the sorrow. He hadn't been able to feel anything beyond his need for this sweet, smart woman.

He owed her far more than sexual release, far more than his thanks.

With a sigh that whispered across his skin, she settled more closely against him. Content. Secure. Trusting.

Her thigh accidentally brushed between his and Edward jerked, wanting her all over again.

"Satisfied that I'm in one piece?" Her drowsy voice was as intimate as a caress.

"Relieved," he answered honestly, surprised to discover she was awake. Maybe that touch hadn't been so accidental, after all. He began to think he'd been had. Drawing light circles against the soft skin of her back, he raised a riot of goose bumps and she shivered.

"Brrr."

"Serves you right." He smiled against her hair. "Spying on me when I'm trying to look my fill of you."

The long, tall vixen sat up, letting the blanket pool

around her hips and exposing every lean, perfect curve to the dappling touch of the firelight. Edward wanted to touch, too. She pulled his hands from her waist and lifted them right up to cover her breasts.

"Seen enough?"

All he could do was shake his head as she straddled him.

The embers between them fanned back to life and burned with equal intensity the second time around. In a glorious conflagration, he thrust himself up inside her and she cried out with a passion that made him feel like a whole man, a talented lover and one lucky son of a gun.

This time, when they finished, he led her to his bedroom and tucked her under the covers on a proper mattress. When he reached for her, she came willingly into his arms.

Edward lay awake in the dark, long after Holly's soft snore told him she'd fallen into a deep sleep.

He was fighting hard to fix his armor back into place, listening for sounds around the perimeter of the house that might indicate anyone who shouldn't be there. He tried to get the tough guy back who could spot the bad guys and keep them at bay long before they got close to the people he cared about. He tried to figure out how strong he could be when she wasn't around to drive him to an AA meeting or listen to his sorrows or talk him out of his fears.

He could call his sponsor, make an appointment with a counselor. Those questions he could answer.

But one problem left him completely stumped. He was in love with Holly Masterson.

What was he supposed to do about that?

Chapter Eleven

"Son of a…"

It was only one of many curses that brought Holly running out of the shower that morning.

"What do you mean, she got cut off? How much do we know?"

Wrapped in a towel and dripping on the throw rug beside Edward's bed, Holly watched him pace from one end of the room to the other, half-dressed and all tense. His handsome face grew more tight and more grim with each step as he dealt with whatever horrible news the caller on his cell phone had to share.

"Yes, I said that to Bill Caldwell." He raked his hair into spiky disarray as the fury worked through him. "I was stirring the pot, trying to get him to show his hand by appealing to his conscience."

His caller made a comment. "Yeah—it worked too well. But he said he loved Mom. I saw the guilt in his eyes, Atticus. He won't hurt her."

At least now she knew it was one of his brothers

calling. Was there a family emergency? A break on their father's case? She was already worried for him. Now she was just plain worried. "Edward?"

He slid his steely glance across the bed, acknowledging her. Then he pointed to her clothes from the night before that he'd folded and laid neatly on the bed. Holly nodded, understanding that she needed to get dressed. Fast. "No, I can't guarantee that. I can't guarantee anything these days. But I swear, he wouldn't do anything to intentionally hurt her."

Edward pulled a T-shirt from the second drawer of his dresser and shrugged into it. With one hand, he tucked it into his jeans. Holly picked up the brown tweed sweater he'd set out and circled around the bed to hand it to him. But he reached for something else instead.

He reached for a box on his closet shelf and pulled out his gun. Glock 9 millimeter. Police issue. He strapped it onto his belt before plucking his sweater from Holly's startled fingers. A man with Edward's background arming himself couldn't be a good thing.

"What's happened?" she mouthed, wishing they had time for morning-after conversation to discuss the closeness they'd shared last night—wishing they had time for any kind of conversation at all.

But Edward had gone into cop mode. No, something harder, more driven, more dangerous than anything she'd seen yet. Maybe she'd never get back the man who'd loved her so well last night, the man who'd opened up his heart to her. Maybe Edward Kincaid couldn't do both anymore. He couldn't be a cop *and* a lover or friend or something more.

Something inside her mourned for the dichotomy within him he couldn't seem to resolve.

Something inside her still hoped.

"Is Holden's team on this? What about Sawyer? Good. Get there. Now. I'm on my way." He had his boots tied on and was striding out to the main room. "Move it, Stick," he ordered, shielding the phone from his command. "I need to drive you to the lab or precinct headquarters."

No way. Not if there was a break in the case. "Where are you going?"

But he didn't hear or wouldn't spare the time to answer. "And you're sure Irina Zorinsky isn't with them?"

Irina Zorinsky? Oh, my God. Holly pulled her jeans down over her boots, ready to get her coat. She could comb through her hair and put on some lipstick in the Jeep. She was ready to leave.

But she paused and went back for one more item she'd seen in the box Edward had pulled from the closet. She slipped the leather wallet into her purse, grabbed her coat and ran out the door after him. She was ankle-deep in snow before she got her coat on. They were speeding and skidding down the long gravel driveway before she had her seat belt on.

"Right. I'll meet you there. We'll get her back." Edward closed his phone and stuffed it into his pocket, putting both hands on the wheel as he pushed on the gas.

"Get who back?"

"My mother. Bill Caldwell kidnapped her."

"KIDNAPPING IS SUCH A STRONG word, Susan." Bill Caldwell kept both hands on the steering wheel as he sped along I-435 north of Kansas City.

"What would you call it?" Her knuckles were white where she gripped the armrest of the car he'd rented for their visit to a local winery in the rolling hills northwest of Kansas City. But John Kincaid's widow was proving as stubborn to reason with as his friend had been eight months earlier. "I ask you to turn the car around and take me home, but you won't. I try to call my sons and tell them you've changed our plans, and you take my phone. Sounds to me like I'm going somewhere against my will."

Bill reached across the seat to take her hand, but she pulled away even from the friendly touch she'd come to accept so readily these past weeks they'd been together. A little frisson of irritation crawled across his skin. True, he hadn't had time to plan this escape the way he wanted. But he was William Caldwell, damn it. She should be grateful for the opportunitity he was giving her to escape the sorrow of these past months.

He'd discovered the remote location where he could stage their "accident." He'd secured male and female cadavers from his research facility and packed them into the trunk. Hopefully they'd burn beyond recognition in the wreck he'd staged and be buried in their place. If not, they'd still be long gone. It was only a hop, skip and a jump to the airport. With the false passports he'd obtained, they'd be on a flight to Hong Kong before the cops even knew they were missing. They'd die, just the way Irina had. And then they'd live their new lives.

"This is a chance for us to have a new start." He eased into the far left lane of the highway to pass a slower-moving vehicle. "We can distance ourselves from the pain of losing John and all the things around us that remind us of him."

"New start? To what? I don't even want to go to the wine-tasting with you anymore."

He bit down on the sharp retort. He'd always admired Susan's levelheadedness, her ability to meet any challenge with her chin held high and a beautifully serene smile on her face. Now that sensibility was keeping her from taking the impulsive leap he'd hoped she would. "It's not as though you'd want for anything, Su. I have money in accounts around the world. We can live anywhere you want."

"I want to live right here in Kansas City." She

shook her head, not comprehending the love he felt for her, nor the danger she'd be in if they turned back now. "My sons are here. I'm a grandmother again, with Sawyer's son and a little one on the way. I don't want to leave them." From the corner of his eye he saw her nostrils flare as she took a deep breath. Then she reached across the seat and touched his arm. She'd defied him and lectured him. And now she thought she could sweet-talk him? "Bill. You and I have been good friends for thirty years. You and John were so close—you've always been family to me."

"I don't want to be *family,* Su. I want to marry you." He took his eyes from the road long enough to condemn the false affection of her touch for the ploy it was. "I'm a good catch."

Understanding his displeasure, she pulled away and fixed her eyes on the highway ahead of them. "I'm not sure I could have gotten through these months since John's murder without you, Bill. Your support, your caring. For that, I will always be grateful. But I don't love you. Not in that way." She gestured out to the bare trees and snow-covered hills as they flew past them. "I under-stand this is a very romantic gesture on your part—to simply drop everything and run away together. Maybe when I was a young woman. But not now. It's two days before Christmas. Our first Christmas without John. My sons and I—our family—we need to be together. Edward is finally showing signs of becoming the man he was before losing Cara and Melinda. If I leave now, he might see it as another loss. He'd blame himself again. I won't do that to my son. Please, Bill. Turn the car around."

"Listen, Su, I'm saving your life!" He pounded the steering wheel, watched her startle and turn pale. "There are people...things you don't know about. But Edward...knows."

"Oh, my God, Bill. No." Her pretty face squinched into a frown of disbelief. And then her cheeks flushed with anger. "Tell me you had nothing to do with John's murder."

"Su—"

"Tell me everything my sons have been telling me about Z Group isn't true."

Bill stared at the gray road ahead of him.

"Tell me you had nothing to do with John's murder!"

He thought of Irina's gloating smile as she'd climbed into the SUV that April night at the river docks. She'd still reeked of blood and gunpowder and death when she dropped John's Z Group ring into his hands and kissed him. *"He's not one of us anymore. He doesn't deserve to wear it."*

With his thumb, Bill turned the gold signet ring on his own finger. John should have listened to him when he'd told his friend to back away from his personal investigation into Z Group. The players were as dangerous today as they'd been during the Cold War.

Yes, he'd been selling technology on the black market through Z Group, as John suspected. Bill would have paid him for his silence, even offered to let him back on the team so he could make more money than any police officer's pension could ever hope to. Bill would have done anything to keep him alive.

But John Kincaid had been an Eagle Scout from day one. How could he face his sons? he'd argued. How could he lead a police department if he took a bribe? He'd warned Bill that he had information that he'd hidden away. John had offered him some bizarre deal that would save his soul and secure their friendship but put Bill away in prison, probably for the rest of his life.

Then Irina had shown up at his office door.

She had no loyalties conflicting her thoughts. She saw everything clearly. The money. The coverup. What needed to be done to save them all.

He hadn't pulled the trigger that killed his friend. "I tried to save John's life."

Susan collapsed in the corner of the seat with an audible gasp. Now she understood what he was trying to save her from. Now she'd come with him.

And then he spotted the big, square vehicle in his rear view mirror, closing in behind them. A giant fist crushed what was left of his soul. "How in the…?"

"Turn the car around, Bill."

He pushed harder on the accelerator.

HOLLY TRIED TO RUB SOME warmth back into her nearly bare fingers as she stood and faced the audience who'd been watching her every move as she and her team processed the two dead bodies in the burned-out car. Edward and his brothers stood on their side of the yellow crime scene tape, as unyielding and unsmiling as the four faces of Mt. Rushmore.

She looked from one grim expression to the next. Her heart was breaking at the fear and speculation that must be twisting them into knots inside. Better keep this clinical if she had any hope of maintaining her professional objectivity. "I can't give you a conclusive answer until I get the vics back in my lab, but—"

"Cut to the chase, Stick." Edward's expression was as cold and detached as she'd ever seen him. "Is it them?"

"I don't think so."

Clouds of warm air masked their faces as they breathed out their relief.

Not everything she had to say was good news. She glanced over at the detective in charge of the scene for approval before she held out the plastic evidence bag she'd already labeled. "But I did find this. Your friends were here."

Atticus reached for it first to study the gold ring inside.

With only latex to keep her fingers warm, Holly shoved her hands beneath her CSI vest and tried to warm them against her body. "I took that off the driver. It has a Cyrillic Z etched on the inside."

"Looks like Dad's fraternity ring," Holden commented.

Atticus adjusted his glasses and looked closer. "Not a fraternity ring. It's a service ring. In this case, I'm guessing it's something the members of Z Group received when they were officially disbanded."

He handed the bag to Sawyer to inspect. "Uncle Bill…" He paused as if saying the name left a bad taste in his mouth. "Bill Caldwell has one like it. I remember him wearing it at Dad's funeral."

Edward took the bag and handed it back to Holly. "And we're sure there are at least two different rings? This isn't a souvenir Bill took off Dad, is it?"

Holden shook his head. "Liza was there that night. She says it was definitely a woman who killed Dad and took the ring and chain off him."

"Speculate all you want," Holly interrupted. "I deal in facts."

"I don't like these facts." Edward's tone was bleak. He was probably still imagining that this was Bill Caldwell and their mother inside the charred vehicle.

"Edward." She tried to touch his hand but he flinched away. She'd like to blame it on the winter chill on her skin, but she recognized the signs of stoic withdrawal. He didn't want to be touched, didn't want to feel comfort—didn't want to feel, period. But she refused to give up on the hurting man locked inside him. "It's not your mother. The arson investigator places the fire late morning or early afternoon. That body has been dead for days."

"Thank God." Holden finally offered her a grateful smile. "Since I talked with Mom just this morning, that can't be her."

"So who are these bodies?" Edward asked. "Where did the ring come from?"

"Offhand, I'd say it was a plant to throw us off the trail. We'll have to check dental records, see if we can retrieve some DNA from the inner tissues, to ID them. But I'm guessing derelicts or bodies donated to science. If your friend Caldwell is involved—"

"He is."

"—then he'd have access to research centers where he could 'borrow' a body. Someone tried to stage their deaths." Holly returned both bags to her kit. "Ultimately, they've just given us more evidence we can evaluate and trace."

"More pieces to fit into the puzzle." Edward's eyes finally focused on her. But he was looking for answers from an M.E., not comfort from a woman who cared. "So, where the hell are Mom and Bill?"

"Mount up, boys." Kevin Grove waved the four uniformed officers on the scene toward their cars. "I think we found them. We've got a situation just a few miles from here at the winery."

"Bill and Mom?"

"A man matching Caldwell's description and two women. One could be your mom." Grove closed his phone and clipped it onto his belt beside his gun. "The other woman is armed with a Makarov nine mil—a European spy weapon."

Edward nodded. "Irina Zorinsky."

"None of you were ever supposed to be working this case." Grove matched eyes with Edward and each of his brothers, all of whom were pulling weapons and checking clips and preparing for battle. "But we're twenty minutes from precinct headquarters and five minutes from the winery. I'm looking for all the backup I can get."

"Edward? Wait." Holly reached into the pocket of her coat and pulled out the leather wallet she'd taken from the box on Edward's bed that morning. She opened it to reveal the KCPD badge inside. "You'll need this."

For a timeless moment, Edward's gaze hardened as he looked down at the symbol of guilt and pain—the symbol of the warrior; of the good, caring man he was inside, as well. Would he take it? Would he reclaim the job—reclaim the man she knew him to be?

Holly held her breath—held his gaze. "Edward?"

And then he snatched the badge from her hand, stuffed it into his coat pocket, and leaned across the yellow crime-scene tape. He caught the side of her neck with his gloved hand and pressed a quick, hot, hard kiss to her mouth. The instant he pulled away, without a single word, he turned and hurried to his Jeep to join the speeding parade of cars kicking up gravel and snow on the country road.

After all five men had driven off into the hills to the north, Holly returned to her bodies and prepped them for transportation to her lab.

She was certain of three things. She loved Edward Kincaid. Loved him so hard it hurt. And he needed her, maybe now more than ever.

And neither Bill Caldwell nor Irina Zorinsky stood a chance against the cadre of armed police officers—of armed Kincaids—heading their way.

"Mom!"

"Su!"

"Drop your weapon! Drop your weapon!"

Twenty minutes of waiting and worrying, bickering and negotiating, threats and empty promises blew up in a matter of seconds when Irina Zorinsky turned her gun on Edward's mother and fired. It had always been her practice to eliminate the threats to her world. She'd already buried a husband, a bastard son, countless employees who'd served their purpose—and one good man who'd been a cop for thirty years and a husband and father for longer than that.

Tonight there were scuffles of guns and furniture, breaking glass, screams and then silence. Edward had simply charged forward from his cover, taking advantage of the momentary chaos and taking charge of the situation. He hoped.

"Oh, God. Edward!"

His mother's gasp tore at his heart, but he couldn't look away from his target. It was up to someone else to pull her out of harm's way. He was taking out the bad guy.

"Kincaid!"

"Ed!"

"He's in it now. Let him work."

The worst thing about a Mexican standoff was that a man had to be able to pull the trigger. He couldn't trust that the other guy—or woman, in this case—wouldn't have the stomach for killing, either, and would drop his gun and walk away.

Edward had no doubt that Irina Zorinsky had the stomach for killing. Bill Caldwell was bleeding out on the floor beside him, having taken the bullet intended for Susan.

"Foolish, foolish man. You'd be nothing without me!"

Irina Zorinsky in the flesh was a beautiful, shapely woman. A throwback to red-lipped movie stars with exotic eyes and expensive tastes. Her lips might be trembling at the sight of her longtime lover and business partner dying with a bullet in his chest, but there was something cold and empty about her eyes. And the hand holding the gun was rock steady.

"You're just like your father, Kincaid. You're the oldest, aren't you? The loose cannon with nothing to lose that my Bill told me about." The tip of her gun was barely a foot from Edward's chin. The tip of his Glock was aimed squarely between her heartless eyes. "He couldn't just let it go. When your father found out that Bill was still using our Z Group connections to turn a profit, he thought he had to do something about it. I had to come all the way from Sarajevo to do what Bill couldn't. I eliminated your father, and I systematically eliminated anyone else who knew the truth. You have no idea how easy it is for a dead woman to wend her way around the world and take care of business that others cannot. And you think *you're* going to stop me?" She laughed.

Edward didn't so much as blink.

Grove was on a radio in the background. There was movement in his peripheral vision. One of the officers on the scene, a good Samaritan, perhaps, was on the floor helping his mother with Bill. He sensed his brothers searching for a location with a clear shot. None was clearer than his own. "You're surrounded. And I'm not moving."

Unfazed by his threat, she smiled. "What about your girlfriend, the doctor? Won't she be very sad when you're gone? You know what it's like to be left behind when a loved one dies, don't you?"

"Don't listen to her, Edward!"

Holly. Edward flinched at the sound of her voice, but didn't dare look away. Damn it. *She* was the good Samaritan, a true doctor, tending to a dying man's wounds. "Get out of here, Stick!"

"I can't. He needs my help. I need to reinflate his chest." She pulled a checkered cloth off a nearby table and guided his mother's hands to press against the hole near Bill's heart.

The two women he loved most in the world were in the line of fire. Again. "Damn it, Holly! Sawyer, Atticus—get them out of here!"

"Where the hell is my S.W.A.T. team?"

"Give me a rifle," Holden commanded.

"No, son. Your shoulder hasn't healed enough for that yet."

"Be strong, Daddy. Grandpa says be strong. I know you can do it."

His daughter's voice centered him. His father's wisdom gave him courage.

"Irina?" he started, in a voice rusty from injury but crystal clear in purpose. "You're under arrest for the murder of Deputy Commissioner John Kincaid."

"HE'S GONE." Ignoring the shouts and movement around them as Kevin Grove demanded backup, Holly reached across Bill Caldwell's body and squeezed Susan Kincaid's hand.

Her gaze darted up to Edward in the middle of

the winery's dining room, standing toe-to-toe with Irina's gun. The woman's aim had been accurate. Despite Bill Caldwell's heroic effort to save a friend or ease a guilty conscience, he'd never really had a chance at surviving. She didn't think she could be more scared than she'd been that night she'd spent in the autopsy chamber, or the night she'd walked in on Edward contemplating a drink. But there was plenty of fear left in her to see the man she loved standing tall with a bullet pointed to his head.

But she had to be strong. She'd been strong for Jillian and her family growing up. Edward needed her to be strong now.

She lowered her gaze to Susan Kincaid. The older woman had been crying, but she was dry-eyed now. The family resemblance to her sons was unmistakable. Other than a few strands of gray, she shared Edward's dark hair. His stubborn jaw must be from his father, but the courage and determination shining from Susan's eyes had been passed on to her oldest son.

"Mrs. Kincaid? You may want to turn away. I'm going to try to retrieve the bullet while it's still fresh— before it begins to decompose. I need it for evidence."

Holly opened her tool kit. When she turned back to the body, Susan was already unbuttoning his jacket and pulling apart his shirt. "I can help."

She heard Edward's voice above the fray. "Irina? You're under arrest—"

And then Holly's phone rang.

"Not now!" She dropped the scalpel and scrambled to retrieve Jillian's phone from her kit. *Unnamed.*

"Holly?"

It rang a second time. *Think, Holly. Figure it out.*

"That jerk." Not her phone. Jillian's. She'd only called one person besides Edward. And he was holding a gun right now, not a phone. *That bastard.* "Damn it, Rick, I know it's you. You and your sick jokes." She answered on the fourth ring. "Rick!"

Her colleague stammered at her accusatory shout. "I was just calling to see why you didn't come in with the bodies. Are you okay?"

"Bull. You're caught, you creep. I'm putting you on report."

And then she was staring at the barrel of a gun.

"TURN OFF THAT DAMN PHONE!" The instant Irina swung her gun toward Holly, Edward attacked.

He'd never punched a woman in his life. Now he had. He couldn't say it felt good to hit her. But it felt damn good to do his job again.

"Somebody get me some handcuffs."

EDWARD BRUSHED THE SNOW off Cara and Melinda's gravestone.

Though a part of his heart would always be buried in the ground beside them, he felt a new growth in his heart. It was a feeling of new life, new hope. And it was nurtured by love and confidence and purpose.

"*Good job, Daddy. Grandpa says so, too.*"

"Thanks, baby. I couldn't have done it without your help to guide me. I love you, baby."

The crunch of snow alerted him to the long-legged woman walking up behind him. Holly had given him some time alone to square things with his family—to say his goodbyes and make his promises for the future.

But now he was eager to move on with his life. Not that every step would go off without a hitch, but for the first time in two years, he was looking forward. And he wasn't as afraid of feeling and living and losing as he'd been before he'd met Holly Masterson.

The twinge in his knee and ankle as he pushed to his feet was just one of those hitches he'd learn to live with. He brushed away the tears freezing on his cheeks and straightened his coat. He adjusted the gun and badge he wore proudly, confidently, on his belt.

He was back to the man he was supposed to be. John Kincaid's oldest son. A testament to his father. A good cop. A good man.

Because of this woman.

He reached for Holly's hand, pulled her to his side, and smiled. "Merry Christmas."

Understanding everything it meant for him to say those words, she smiled back and answered, "I love you, too."

Epilogue

Edward Kincaid had lived through some scary things in his life. He'd held his daughter as she died. He'd stood up in an AA meeting and told a group of strangers that he was an alcoholic. He'd seen the woman he loved raise her chin defiantly as a murderer aimed a gun at her head.

Yet walking up to his mother's front door on Christmas Eve had to be about the scariest thing he'd ever done.

But he had a promise to keep.

Besides, the strong woman beside him had been most insistent. Part of the healing process, she'd said. Holly had been right about so many things— what he could do, who he could be. She'd been right about how to catch a killer and finally close the book on his father's murder. Justice for his family had been a long time coming. It wasn't as good as having his wise, loving father here to guide him. It didn't take away the pain of knowing a lifelong friend had betrayed his entire family. But knowing William Caldwell was dead and Irina Zorinsky would pay for the lives she'd taken helped ease the Kincaid's loss.

Holly had known they could heal—Sawyer and Melissa and their son, Atticus and Brooke, Holden and Liza, Susan Kincaid. Even a beat-up son of a gun like him could. And they *would* heal, given enough time.

But damn, this was hard.

"Come on, Lieutenant." Holly nudged him onto the front porch when his steps slowed. "Your family wants to see you."

Edward reached for the doorbell but hesitated as a flurry of activity crashed through the interior of the house. "Is that a dog barking?"

"More than one, from the sound of things."

A little boy squealed. A mother's warning softened into laughter and was joined by the deep voices of men.

He felt Holly's hand at the small of his back, urging him forward. "Go on."

Edward turned to face her, stroking her jaw with his gloved fingers, willing her to understand. "I abandoned those people inside. It took my father's death to fish me out of a bottle and get me to even talk to them. My arrival might kill their celebration."

She smiled. That wise, beautiful curve of her lips that had always soothed him. "It might kill *you* if you don't walk through that door." She leaned in and kissed him with those beautiful lips. "Ring the doorbell. It'll be the bravest thing you've ever done."

And so he did. After a beat of silence, the happy crowd inside seemed to rush the door. Edward quickly reached back to grab Holly's hand and hold on tight for support.

His mother opened the door. She wore the same holiday apron he remembered from his childhood. His brothers stood behind her. A wink from Holden. Nods of approval from Sawyer and Atticus. Beyond them, the commotion continued. Sawyer's pregnant wife chased their toddler son through the foyer. A trio of dogs trotted behind, followed by a freckle-faced redhead trying to get their attention. A quiet beauty, with glasses and long hair, stopped to offer a shy wave before hurrying after the rest of the parade.

The people were grown. Different. But the feeling was familiar.

"Edward." Susan Kincaid threw her arms around her oldest son's neck and hugged him tight. Her tears warmed his neck before she pulled away. "Welcome home, son. Holly?" She gave Stick a hug as well. "Merry Christmas. Welcome."

"Merry Christmas."

Edward wasn't sure how to say this, but suddenly, a calm washed over him. He reached into his pocket.

"I brought you a gift, Mom."

"Oh, Edward. Having you here is the only gift I need."

"Eight months ago, on the day we buried Dad, you asked me to do something for you." Edward reached into his pocket, squeezing Holly's hand even tighter as his mother waited expectantly. "Irina Zorinsky ruined a lot of lives. And apparently, she took perverse pleasure in collecting a sick memento from each of those lives. Kevin Grove searched her luggage at the airport and—"

"Oh, honey, I don't want to even discuss that woman. Not today."

"You'll want this." He flipped open the wallet to reveal the KCPD badge that he'd lovingly polished that morning. "It's Dad's. Merry Christmas."

Susan Kincaid burst into tears and hugged him again. As his brothers piled on and joined the group embrace, Edward looked over and winked at Holly. She was smiling.

God, he loved that woman.

Loved this family.

Loved being a cop. Loved being alive.

Yeah. It was about time he came home.

* * * * *

Here is a sneak preview of
A STONE CREEK CHRISTMAS,
the latest in Linda Lael Miller's acclaimed
MCKETTRICK *series.*

A lonely horse brought vet Olivia O'Ballivan
to Tanner Quinn's farm, but it's the rancher's
love that might cause her to stay.

A STONE CREEK CHRISTMAS
Available December 2008
from Silhouette Special Edition.

Tanner heard the rig roll in around sunset. Smiling, he wandered to the window. Watched as Olivia O'Ballivan climbed out of her Suburban, flung one defiant glance toward the house and started for the barn, the golden retriever trotting along behind her.

Taking his coat and hat down from the peg next to the back door, he put them on and went outside. He was used to being alone, even liked it, but keeping company with Doc O'Ballivan, bristly though she sometimes was, would provide a welcome diversion.

He gave her time to reach the horse Butterpie's stall, then walked into the barn.

The golden retriever came to greet him, all wagging

tail and melting brown eyes, and he bent to stroke her soft, sturdy back. "Hey, there, dog," he said.

Sure enough, Olivia was in the stall, brushing Butterpie down and talking to her in a soft, soothing voice that touched something private inside Tanner and made him want to turn on one heel and beat it back to the house.

He'd be damned if he'd do it, though.

This was *his* ranch, *his* barn. Well-intentioned as she was, *Olivia* was the trespasser here, not him.

"She's still very upset," Olivia told him, without turning to look at him or slowing down with the brush.

Shiloh, always an easy horse to get along with, stood contentedly in his own stall, munching away on the feed Tanner had given him earlier. Butterpie, he noted, hadn't touched her supper as far as he could tell.

"Do you know anything at all about horses, Mr. Quinn?" Olivia asked.

He leaned against the stall door, the way he had the day before, and grinned. He'd practically been raised on horseback; he and Tessa had grown up on their grandmother's farm in the Texas hill country, after their folks divorced and went their separate ways, both of them too busy to bother with a couple of kids. "A few things," he said. "And I mean to call you Olivia, so you might as well return the favor and address me by my first name."

He watched as she took that in, dealt with it, decided on an approach. He'd have to wait and see what that turned out to be, but he didn't mind. It was a pleasure just watching Olivia O'Ballivan grooming a horse.

"All right, *Tanner,*" she said. "This barn is a disgrace. When are you going to have the roof fixed? If it snows again, the hay will get wet and probably mold…"

He chuckled, shifted a little. He'd have a crew out there the following Monday morning to replace the roof and shore up the walls—he'd made the arrangements over a week before—but he felt no particular compunction to explain that. He was enjoying her ire too much; it made her color rise and her hair fly when she turned her head, and the faster breathing made her perfect breasts go up and down in an enticing rhythm. "What makes you so sure I'm a greenhorn?" he asked mildly, still leaning on the gate.

At last she looked straight at him, but she didn't move from Butterpie's side. "Your hat, your boots—that fancy red truck you drive. I'll bet it's customized."

Tanner grinned. Adjusted his hat. "Are you telling me real cowboys don't drive red trucks?"

"There are lots of trucks around here," she said. "Some of them are red, and some of them are new. And *all* of them are splattered with mud or manure or both."

"Maybe I ought to put in a car wash, then," he teased. "Sounds like there's a market for one. Might be a good investment."

She softened, though not significantly, and spared him a cautious half smile, full of questions she probably wouldn't ask. "There's a good car wash in Indian Rock," she informed him. "People go there. It's only forty miles."

"Oh," he said with just a hint of mockery. "*Only* forty miles. Well, then. Guess I'd better dirty up my truck if I want to be taken seriously in these here parts. Scuff up my boots a bit, too, and maybe stomp on my hat a couple of times."

Her cheeks went a fetching shade of pink. "You are twisting what I said," she told him, brushing Butterpie again, her touch gentle but sure. "I meant…"

Tanner envied that little horse. Wished he had a furry hide, so he'd need brushing, too.

"You *meant* that I'm not a real cowboy," he said. "And you could be right. I've spent a lot of time on construction sites over the last few years, or in meetings where a hat and boots wouldn't be appropriate. Instead of digging out my old gear, once I decided to take this job, I just bought new."

"I bet you don't even *have* any old gear," she challenged, but she was smiling, albeit cautiously, as though she might withdraw into a disapproving frown at any second.

He took off his hat, extended it to her. "Here,"

he teased. "Rub that around in the muck until it suits you."

She laughed, and the sound—well, it caused a powerful and wholly unexpected shift inside him. Scared the hell out of him and, paradoxically, made him yearn to hear it again.

* * * * *

Discover how this rugged rancher's wanderlust is tamed in time for a merry Christmas, in
A STONE CREEK CHRISTMAS.
In stores December 2008.

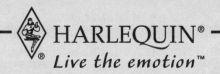

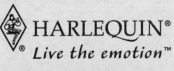

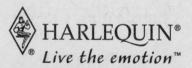

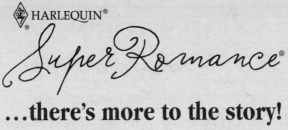
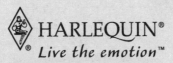

HARLEQUIN®
Presents®

**The world's bestselling romance series...
The series that brings you your favorite authors,
month after month:**

Helen Bianchin...Emma Darcy
Lynne Graham...Penny Jordan
Miranda Lee...Sandra Marton
Anne Mather...Carole Mortimer
Melanie Milburne...Michelle Reid

and many more talented authors!

Wealthy, powerful, gorgeous men...
Women who have feelings just like your own...
The stories you love, set in exotic, glamorous locations...

HARLEQUIN®
Presents®

Seduction and Passion Guaranteed!

HPDIR08